Living Proof
Evangelism

Cultivating a Lifestyle

of Sharing Your Faith

PARTICIPANT'S GUIDE

ZondervanPublishingHouse
Grand Rapids, Michigan

A Division of HarperCollinsPublishers

CBMC
**CHRISTIAN BUSINESS
MEN'S COMMITTEE**

Living Proof: Evangelism Participant's Guide
Copyright © 1990 by The Christian Business Men's Committee USA

First Zondervan edition, 1997

Requests for information should be addressed to:

ZondervanPublishingHouse
Grand Rapids, Michigan 49530

ISBN: 0-310-21360-6

The Christian Business Men's Committee is an international evangelical organization of Christian business and professional men whose primary purpose is to present Jesus Christ as Savior and Lord to other business and professional men and to train these men to carry out the Great Commission (Matthew 28:18-20; Colossians 1:28-29).

CBMC of USA is a nondenominational, nonprofit Christian ministry supported by gifts from people committed to reaching and discipling business and professional men for Jesus Christ. More information may be obtained by writing or calling:

Christian Business Men's Committee of USA
1800 MaCallie Avenue
Chattanooga, TN 37404
615-698-4444

Interior illustrations: Bob Fuller

Printed in the United States of America

99 00 01 02 03 /❖ ML/ 10 9 8

Contents

Christian Business Men's Committee of USA

From its founding in 1930, the Christian Business Men's Committee has been an effective ministry for Jesus Christ in the marketplace. Today, over 12,000 members are dedicated to presenting the gospel and helping Christians grow in their faith.

CBMC's commitment to evangelism brought about the development of the Lifestyle Evangelism Seminar in 1982. The objective of this ten-hour training session is to help Christians understand that evangelism is not simply a one-time event, but a process of helping a person come *one step closer* to a relationship with Jesus Christ.

Since its inception, CBMC's Lifestyle Evangelism Seminar has trained and equipped nearly 50,000 Christians around the globe in the principles and processes of lifestyle evangelism. Over 400 leaders are certified to lead these seminars, which God has used to revolutionize the way we present the gospel.

Because the Lifestyle Evangelism Seminar requires a ten-hour commitment and a trained leader, it is not always convenient for everyone to attend. But now, the principles and processes of lifestyle evangelism are available for individuals and small groups in the form of *Living Proof.*

What Is This Series About?

Bill and Jackie Warner

Gerry and Linda Sanders

Most of us who know Jesus Christ want the people we care about to know Him, too. But few of us find that introducing our friends to the King of the universe is easy. In fact, many of us leave evangelism on the shelf until we've mastered the simpler aspects of life in Christ—like treating our families with sacrificial love, or handling our finances with radical faith!

The good news is that, just as grace and hope are available for simple impossibilities like love and faith, they are also available for drawing unbelievers to Christ. That's what this series is about: grace and hope. You'll find hope as you

- understand some basic truths about how to reach out, and
- team up with others with similar feelings to think and pray.

You'll find grace—God's empowering, unconditional presence—as you take some first steps in venturing out into your world.

How the Series Works
There are twelve sessions in this series, and we recommend you cover them in twelve weeks.

Each session should take about ninety minutes, although you can expand or compress the session as you see fit. You'll open with a question or two, then view an approximately fifteen-minute-long video segment, then follow with discussion questions and workshop exercises, and finish with prayer. To take home, you'll have an action project, an optional mini-Bible study to whet your appetite for the next session, and sometimes an optional article that expands on the current session. (This sounds like a lot, but homework may take as little as fifteen minutes a week.)

The video is no dull lecture; it's full of memorable characters, humor, and some scenes that may startle you. Each week you will join a group of people much like yourselves—people who love God and want to share His message of love and reconciliation with those around them, but who also approach faith-sharing with many of the same fears, and lack of time and skill, that confront you. We hope you'll find the video segments and the discussions that follow to be two of the most fun learning experiences you've ever had.

Twelve main characters carry the story from week to week.

Steve Lunsford

Walt and Anne Ridgeway

Hayden and Delores Bishop

Marjorie Calloway

Nick Pirecas

Phil Rasouske

Bill Warner is a forty-three-year-old middle manager. He was raised a nominal Christian but only discovered in his thirties how good the good news is. His wife, *Jackie,* has been a serious Christian all of her life. She believes her main calling is to make a home for Bill and her sons, Billy junior and Scotty.

Gerry Sanders is on the fast track to the top of a Fortune 500 company. He had a bad experience with Christianity as a youth and wants no part of it. *Linda,* his wife, wants to be content with this second marriage (her first ended in divorce), but the emptiness of money and career are beginning to get to her. Gerry and Linda are new neighbors of the Warners.

Steve Lunsford, an engineer in his late forties, has been committed to lifestyle evangelism for years. He's training a group of his Christian friends to reach their friends with the gospel; Bill and Jackie are part of that group.

Walt Ridgeway heads U.S. operations for a multi-national computer technology firm. He's a long-time Christian but also a recovering alcoholic. He joined Steve's group to learn to give away what he's gotten from Jesus. His wife, *Anne,* spends two mornings each week as a parent volunteer at the high school.

Hayden Bishop is a partner in a general law firm and an elder in his church. He's quite biblically knowledgeable, but he's in Steve's group to learn because he realized how many people he alienated over the years by a too-strict outlook on life. *Delores,* his wife, has put up with a lot from him and their kids, but she's mellowed rather than hardened. She grew up in a pastor's household, has seen and heard it all, and still loves Jesus.

Marjorie Calloway is in management in a printing company. Her mother was a great lady of faith, but Marjorie had to sample the big world for a lot of years before she returned to the foundation she received as a child. She's also in Steve's group.

Nick Pirecas, the youngest member of the group, is still recovering from a shocking divorce of two years ago. He came to Christ in college and has spent time with a parachurch missions team in Central America, but he's not all that grounded in the Bible. He works for Walt's company, writing custom software for major corporate clients.

Phil Rasouske was Gerry's closest friend and drinking buddy in Viet Nam, where he received the nickname "Raz." When he arrives to stay with the Sanders during a business trip, Bill and Jackie are in for some rude awakenings.

The Culture Gap

It's hard to communicate with someone who speaks a different language. And even though we've grown up in the same neighborhoods and have watched the same TV programs, we Christians speak a remarkably different language from the nonChristians around us. We may use the same words, but the core beliefs and values behind those words are worlds apart. The purposes of this session are

- to examine the differences between the Christian and nonChristian cultures in North America,
- to discover why these differences can become barriers to communicating the gospel, and
- to start learning how to get past those barriers.

WARM UP

(20 minutes)

Your reasons for taking this course may stem from a variety of motives. Perhaps you have a burning love for your unbelieving neighbors or coworkers. Perhaps you want to get past the guilt and frustration of failure. You may even be here because someone dragged you to the group. And, depending on your reason, you may be wondering whether or not this course will be worth your time. The aims of this warm-up session are to convince you that this course *is* worth your time and to begin building you together as a group that can support each other as you wade into unfamiliar waters.

1. a. Group survey: How many of you came to Christ as a result of

   ❑ some type of crusade in a church, auditorium, or stadium?
   ❑ an evangelistic appeal over television or radio?
   ❑ a personal relationship with one or more ordinary believers, including family members?

   b. What does this poll tell you about how to reach the world for Christ in today's culture?

The greatest barriers to evangelism are not theological, they are cultural.
(Joe Aldrich, *Life-Style Evangelism*)

2. Take one minute to tell the group how God became more than just a word to you. Include one of the biggest barriers you had to overcome in letting God be real in your life. (Example: I didn't want to give up certain of my favorite habits.)

3. What are the biggest barriers that hinder you from effectively sharing your faith with nonbelieving friends?

Your Barriers

Barriers Shared by Others
in Your Group

 VIDEO

(20 minutes)

You are about to join a group of believers who are learning how to share their faith in today's world. You will discover some of the *cultural differences* between Christians and nonChristians that make reaching out even to next-door neighbors a cross-cultural experience.

Our story opens with a glimpse of a growing friendship between Bill, a Christian, and Gerry, his nonChristian next-door neighbor. (You can find their photos on pages 5-6 and some information about them on page 6.) Bill and Gerry haven't known each other very long, but Bill has a strong desire to draw his friend to Christ. Notice the differences in the way they each look at life.

Next we'll follow Bill and his wife, Jackie, and their friends as they gather for the first night of a learning group much like yours.

Be a participant! Take notes so that you can build on their conversation in your own discussion after the video. We've provided plenty of space for your notes and some hints about key issues.

Now get ready to turn on the video. As you watch, think about these questions:

How accurately does this segment reflect our culture?
What is your initial reaction when confronted with the differences between believers and unbelievers?

TURN ON VIDEO

FROM THE VIDEO

The differences between believers and unbelievers are vast.

Differences Between Believers and Unbelievers
• *Values* about money, time, priorities, personal conduct, sexual behavior, honesty.
• *Philosophy* behind those values:

What's the authority for truth? (God? Science? Law? Nothing?)

Who's in charge? (God? Me? Nobody?)

Why am I here?

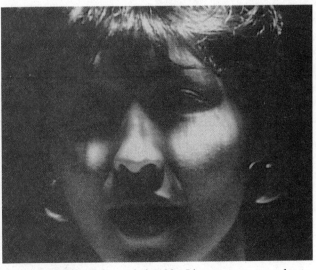

"If I'm stifled in a job or relationship, I have to regroup and get out. It's that simple."

"What's the big deal if you wait until you're married or not? . . . If you love someone. . . ."

"The right grades plus the right test scores equals the right school, which equals the right job, which equals success, period."

However, there's hope. What we have in *common* makes it possible for us to reach unbelievers with the good news of Jesus Christ. All human beings are

- made in _____ _____ and

- corrupted by _____.

Guilt follows sin. And guilt creates openness to the gospel. Why?

ON THE VIDEO

(20 minutes)

4. How accurately do you think this segment portrays our culture?

5. What is your initial reaction when confronted with the differences between believers and unbelievers? (Select as many responses as apply, or substitute your own.)

❏ enthusiastic expectation
❏ hope
❏ determination
❏ concern
❏ fear
❏ retreat
❏ hopelessness

6. What are the worldview, values, and therefore, behavior of secular man? Of biblical man? Fill in this chart.

Man is made in God's image; therefore he has a natural receptivity to spiritual truth. All evangelism is predicated on this fact.
(Jim Petersen, *Living Proof*)

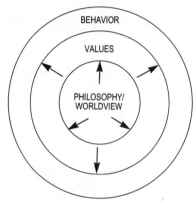

Behavior reflects our values. Values flow out of our worldview (basic philosophy or outlook).

SECULAR MAN	BIBLICAL MAN
Worldview: • I am the center of my world. • I am the product of matter, time, and chance. • I don't know if I have any purpose other than what I give myself. • God is either nonexistent or an impersonal force.	**Worldview:** • God is the center of my world. • I am created by an infinite God who relates to me personally. • I exist to know and love Jesus Christ and to make Him known to a lost world. • God is a wise and good personal Being, my Creator.
Values: • There are no moral absolutes. • I live to advance myself materially or spiritually. • Eat, drink, and be merry, for tomorrow we die. • Other (e.g., time, money, career, relationships):	**Values:** • God's Word reveals absolutes. • Glorifying God takes priority over my desires. • Loving my neighbor takes priority over my desires. • Other:
Behavior:	**Behavior:**

7. Why would it be hard to explain the gospel to someone who believed these statements?

   a. Gerry: "I'll be fine. I'm better than this [obstacle]. There's only one thing I need, and it's tall and cold and I want it right now."

   b. "Life is just going from experience to experience."

   c. "The right job equals success, period."

   d. "My truth is as good as your truth. If you think you can claim any special knowledge, you're not just kidding yourself, you're dangerous."

8. What might make a guy like Gerry receptive to the gospel, despite his worldview and values?

Life is like the butterflies. They spend their time flitting from flower to flower. When it's over, it's over. The idea is to look as pretty as you can while you flit.
(Secularized Man)

(Optional)

Think of the unbelievers where you live and work.

• What are some of their habits, values, or attitudes about life that *hinder* them from understanding or being drawn to the gospel?

• What feelings or desires might they have that would give the Holy Spirit a point of access in their lives?

LOOKING UPWARD

(5 minutes)

In this session, you've identified some strong cultural barriers against the gospel, but also some even stronger reasons for hope. God has designed men and women—even the tough nuts in your world—to be reachable.

Maybe you're encouraged; perhaps you're still apprehensive; maybe you're just confused. Spend the last five minutes of the session looking to the One who sent you on this mission in the first place: God.

9. Divide into pairs (preferably with someone other than your spouse). Take turns with your partner telling God how you feel right now about being His messenger: "God, I feel like . . . ." You can tell Him about your hopes and concerns, about your unbelieving friends—whatever is on your heart.

Then close by thanking God for one thing you've learned in this session. You might thank Him for putting spiritual receptors into each person's heart, or for offering you a chance to participate with Him in reaching your friends.

If you like, you can also ask for the discernment to understand your friends and the wisdom to approach them as Jesus would. Invite the Holy Spirit to begin working in their lives.

ACTION STEPS

Watch. This week, watch a prime-time television show, including commercials. As you watch, answer the following questions and be prepared to share your answers with your group in the next session.

• What do the characters in the show value? What is important to them?

• What would be their response to the question "Why are you (we) here on earth?"

• Think about the commercials. What do you sense the sponsors feel *you* need or value?

Listen. Ask one or more unbelievers this question: "What would you say is your main purpose in life?" Listen attentively to the answer. Then thank them (without giving your own view, unless they really seem to want to know) for revealing something personal and letting you learn something valuable. Even if they brush off the question or say they've never thought about it, that in itself says something about their outlook.

Also, try to be generally aware of the beliefs and values of the unbelievers around you. Notice advertisements and magazine covers. Listen to the feelings and opinions people express.

Read. On pages 14-17 is an article summarizing how *secularization* has affected our culture, and how God has provided a way to reach unbelievers despite secularization. The article is condensed from chapters 1 and 2 of *Living Proof* by Jim Petersen. Read it in preparation for your next session.

BIBLE STUDY

In this session you examined the cultural gap between believers and unbelievers. In session 2 you will go deeper and observe the spiritual gap. To prepare for that discussion, read Ephesians 2:1-10 sometime during the coming week. In the following chart, write down what this passage says about the spiritual states of those who are "in Christ" and those who are not.

As for you, you were dead in your transgressions and sins, in which you used to live when you followed the ways of this world and of the ruler of the kingdom of the air, the spirit who is now at work in those who are disobedient. All of us also lived among them at one time, gratifying the cravings of our sinful nature and following its desires and thoughts. Like the rest, we were by nature objects of wrath. But because of his great love for us, God, who is rich in mercy, made us alive with Christ even when we were dead in transgressions—it is by grace you have been saved. And God raised us up with Christ and seated us with him in the heavenly realms in Christ Jesus, in order that in the coming ages he might show the incomparable riches of his grace, expressed in his kindness to us in Christ Jesus. For it is by grace you have been saved, through faith—and this not from yourselves, it is the gift of God—not by works, so that no one can boast. For we are God's workmanship, created in Christ Jesus to do good works, which God prepared in advance for us to do.

(Ephesians 2:1-10)

NOT "IN CHRIST"	"IN CHRIST"

How might this contrast affect the way you approach unbelievers?

UNDERSTANDING OUR GENERATION

There were once "men of Issachar, who understood the times and knew what Israel should do" (1 Chronicles 12:32).

Men of Issachar, where are you now?

The Gap

A hundred years ago, believers and unbelievers in Western culture agreed about most of the basic issues of life. Almost everybody believed God existed, was a Person, had created the world, and had established certain moral standards reflected in the Bible. But about a century ago a cultural gap began to crack that consensus, and it's been widening ever since.

First, Darwin and other scientists challenged the idea that a God created the world. Believers and unbelievers began to differ over a basic question of life: "How did I get here?" Science became so chic that people started applying the scientific method to just about everything, including God. Since He wouldn't stand still to be weighed and measured, He was erased as a theory.

Scientists declared that people were simply the product of chance and natural selection. Well, philosophers reasoned, if that's true, then the *purpose* for our existence is in doubt. We aren't here because a loving God created us with a plan. So philosophers opened up a second question: "Why am I here?"

As people questioned their origin and purpose, a third explosion widened the cultural gap even further. If the God of the Bible no longer gave us existence and purpose, then the Bible's moral standards should be scrapped, too. The question "How, then, should I live?" was up for grabs. This issue has burned for decades, until by now most people are convinced that absolute truth (including moral truth) does not exist. Right and wrong have been replaced by "do your own thing." Self has become god.

THE CAUSE OF THE CHASM

80-100 years ago, Western culture had a consensus on the basic issues of life. . . . There was a unified worldview.

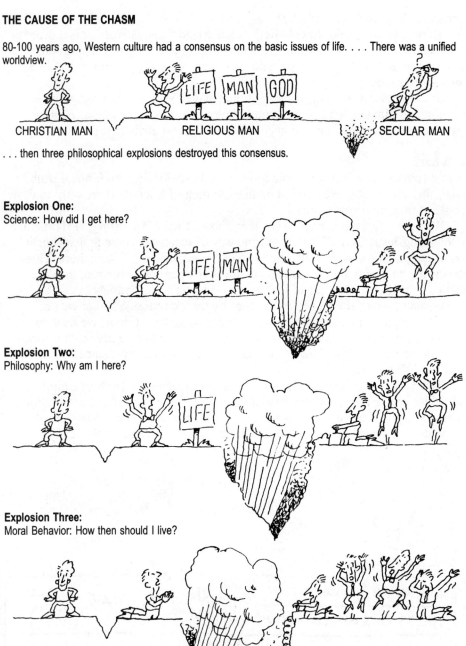

CHRISTIAN MAN RELIGIOUS MAN SECULAR MAN

. . . then three philosophical explosions destroyed this consensus.

Explosion One:
Science: How did I get here?

Explosion Two:
Philosophy: Why am I here?

Explosion Three:
Moral Behavior: How then should I live?

Secularization and the New Age

We call people who hold these beliefs "secularized." *Secularization* is a process by which religious ideas become "less meaningful and religious institutions more marginal."[1] It is contagious, and no one in our society—not even Christians—is immune.

But secularization is only a transitional stage. Man abhors a religious vacuum, and already our culture is moving toward mystical Eastern religions, conscious self-worship, and the occult. Secularization drifts into the New Age.

So What?

What difference does all this make to us, who base our lives on biblical truth? It makes this difference: We need to be like the men of Issachar if we want to draw people of this culture to Christ.

We want people to answer "How then should I live?" by saying, "I should live by following Jesus Christ." But there is no way a person can come to that conclusion as long as his answers to the first two questions are that of our culture. Those answers are so deeply rooted that they aren't even open for discussion; they're mostly unconscious. They are of the "everybody knows . . ." variety.

Human beings are shaped to the core by their culture. Whether we are taking the gospel to a Japanese or the secularized guy next door, we have to communicate in language he can understand. We have to take his basic assumptions into account—things like "Truth is relative," "I exist by chance," and "God is the Undifferentiated All."

Reaching our neighbors is a cross-cultural experience. Their assumptions and values are as foreign to our biblical views as those of a tribe that worships ancestors. If we presume that people are people and talk to our coworkers about repentance, we are in for a shock. The word isn't even in their vocabulary.

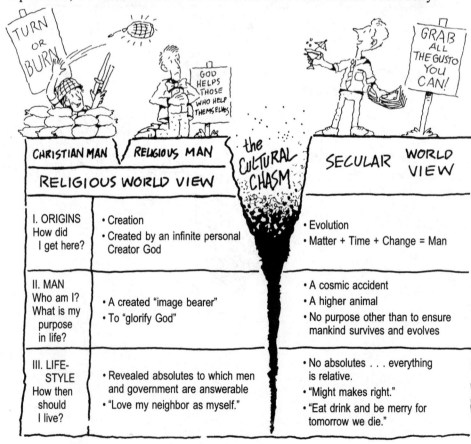

CHRISTIAN MAN	RELIGIOUS MAN	SECULAR WORLD VIEW	
RELIGIOUS WORLD VIEW			
I. ORIGINS How did I get here?	• Creation • Created by an infinite personal Creator God	• Evolution • Matter + Time + Change = Man	
II. MAN Who am I? What is my purpose in life?	• A created "image bearer" • To "glorify God"	• A cosmic accident • A higher animal • No purpose other than to ensure mankind survives and evolves	
III. LIFE-STYLE How then should I live?	• Revealed absolutes to which men and government are answerable • "Love my neighbor as myself."	• No absolutes . . . everything is relative. • "Might makes right." • "Eat drink and be merry for tomorrow we die."	

Built-in Receptors

Is it hopeless, then? That's often our first sense when we find ourselves surrounded by people we do not understand. We may prefer to ignore cultural differences because we don't know how to work with them. But besides being shaped by culture, all people have two other things in common that make them susceptible to the gospel no matter what their culture: They are made in God's image, and they are fallen.

Man is created in God's image. God has made man unique, significant, and Godlike in certain ways. He is able to relate to God as person to Person. He is conscious of himself and is able to make moral choices. And there is something within man that keeps him struggling with the riddle of his own consciousness—until he acknowledges God. This drive is a built-in receptor for spiritual truth.

Man is fallen. When he fell, three calamities occurred:

- He came to know good and evil.
- His life became futile.
- He encountered death.

The knowledge of good and evil shifted man from God-centeredness to self-centeredness (Genesis 3:5,22). Self-centeredness gave birth to shame and guilt—man estranged from himself, from others, and from God. But these become another receptor for the gospel. Man's conscience prods him to find a solution to shame and guilt.

Futility makes life a pointless struggle (Genesis 3:17-19, Ecclesiastes 2:22-23). We expend our lives just managing to exist. Then it is back to dust. But the desperate pain of futility drives us to the question "Why am I doing all this?" and urges us to seek reconciliation with a God who gives meaning to life.

At the Fall, man died in every sense of the word. In his relationships, in his spirit, it was sudden death. His physical death was slower. Man resists death with everything he has. He is obsessed with fear of it. He just cannot make peace with the idea of mortality. Why? Because God has set immortality in our hearts (Ecclesiastes 3:11). This flight from death and longing for endless life provides another receptor for the gospel.

These built-in receptors provide common ground between believer and unbeliever and give us hope that even stubborn hearts can be reached. We can face our neighbor's cultural barriers, knowing that they are not the whole story.

If we are to be effective ambassadors for the true King, we must understand and care about the people to whom we are sent. Grieve for them: they have been trained since birth to believe falsehood and are surrounded by those who agree with them, but their beliefs are a dead end. It will take something drastic for them to turn their back on what "everybody" believes. Something drastic like a love that understands.

For Further Reading

Jim Petersen, *Living Proof,* chapters 1-6.
Joe Aldrich, *Life-Style Evangelism*, introduction, chapter 3.
Joe Aldrich, *Gentle Persuasion*, introduction, chapter 1.
Richard Peace, *Small Group Evangelism*, chapter 1.
Rebecca Pippert, *Out of the Saltshaker and into the World*, chapter 1.

NOTE
1. Os Guinness, *The Gravedigger File* (London: Hodder and Stoughton, 1983), pages 52-53.

Our Spiritual Resources

The cultural gap between believers and unbelievers is not the only barrier that challenges us. Even more formidable is the spiritual gap between unbelievers and God. But we're not left to our own abilities. In this session we'll

- explore what this spiritual gap is, and
- identify the resources God uses to bridge the chasm.

WARM UP
(15 minutes)

1. Share what you learned from watching prime-time television this week.

    a. What values were displayed by the characters or writers in the program?

    b. What values did the commercial sponsors assume or hope you (the viewer) have?

2. (Optional) What conclusions did you draw from the mini-Bible study on Ephesians 2:1-10?

3. (Optional) What insights did you gain from the article "Understanding Our Generation"?

4. Think of an unbeliever you know. On your own, complete the following questionnaire as you think that person would answer it.

The god of this age has *blinded* the minds of unbelievers, so that they cannot see the light of the gospel of the glory of Christ, who is the image of God.
(2 Corinthians 4:4, emphasis added)

"The Spirit of the Lord is on me,
    because he has anointed me
    to preach good news to the poor.
He has sent me to proclaim freedom for
    the prisoners
    and recovery of sight for the blind,
to release the oppressed,
    to proclaim the year of the Lord's
    favor."

(Luke 4:18-19)

As for you, you were *dead* in your transgressions and sins, in which you used to live when you followed the ways of this world and of the ruler of the kingdom of the air, the spirit who is now at work in those who are disobedient. All of us also lived among them at one time, *gratifying the cravings of our sinful nature* and following its desires and thoughts. Like the rest, we were by nature *objects of wrath.*
(Ephesians 2:1-3, emphasis added)

For he has rescued us from the dominion of *darkness* and brought us into the kingdom of the Son he loves. . . . Once you were *alienated* from God and were *enemies* in your minds because of your evil behavior.
(Colossians 1:13,21; emphasis added)

What does it take to break someone out of this prison?

a. I think I'm . . .

❑ lost   ❑ on track
❑ spiritually poor   ❑ doing fine
❑ imprisoned/captive   ❑ free
❑ blind to reality   ❑ aware of reality
❑ dead in sin   ❑ alive and growing
❑ under God's wrath   ❑ not under God's wrath
❑ in the dark   ❑ in the light
❑ without hope   ❑ full of hope

b. Now share with your group whether you think your friend's answers would fall mainly in the left or right column.

c. If you were giving your opinions on your friend's life, would you place him mainly in the left or right column?

d. How do you think your friend would respond if you tried to convince her that the left column was her true condition?

 VIDEO

(20 minutes)

In this segment, Steve's evangelism training group confronts the spiritual gap between God and the unbeliever. We'll also get another taste of the gap between believer and unbeliever as we flash back to the day Bill and Gerry first met. As you watch this segment, consider this question:

What's it like to live in a spiritual prison?

_____
TURN ON VIDEO
_____

FROM THE VIDEO

The unbelievers are in a *spiritual prison*, and the good news is that Jesus came to rescue them from that prison. But there's a catch: Unbelievers don't see their prison, and they often feel rejected if a believer talks about it.

So, because they're spiritually blinded by "the god of this world," they can be reached only through *supernatural power*. God has chosen to use the following resources.

God's Resources for Evangelism
• *The Holy Spirit,* who works through inner conviction and circumstances;
• *The Bible,* which testifies to the truth; and
• *The believer,* who lives the truth, speaks the truth, and prays.

ON THE VIDEO

(30 minutes)

5. From what you've seen in the video and your own experience, what's it like to live in a spiritual prison? For instance, what happens to a person's

   • sense of right and wrong?
   • priorities?
   • relationships?
   • perception of reality?
   • self-esteem?

6. Why does it take supernatural power to free someone from a spiritual prison like this?

7. As an enthusiastic new convert, the Apostle Paul was driven out of town because of his aggressive style of evangelism. Paul won all the arguments but made few converts. What did he eventually learn he needed and didn't need in order to bring people into God's Kingdom (1 Corinthians 2:1-5)?

NEEDED	DIDN'T NEED

8. What do you think it means in practical terms to rely on "a demonstration of the Spirit's power" (1 Corinthians 2:4) in reaching unbelievers?

For it is by grace you have been saved, through faith—and this not from yourselves, it is the gift of God.
(Ephesians 2:8)

Many unbelievers don't even understand what the fight is all about.

When I came to you, brothers, *I did not come with eloquence or superior wisdom* as I proclaimed to you the testimony about God. For I resolved to know nothing while I was with you except Jesus Christ and him crucified. I came to you in weakness and fear, and with much trembling. My message and my preaching were *not with wise and persuasive words, but with a demonstration of the Spirit's power,* so that your faith might not rest on men's wisdom, but on God's power.
(1 Corinthians 2:1-5, emphasis added)

When he [the Holy Spirit] comes, he will convict the world of guilt in regard to sin and righteousness and judgment.

(John 16:8)

9. In your experience, how does the Holy Spirit go about convicting someone, as John 16:8 describes?

(In sessions 9 and 10 we'll explore the Bible's role as a supernatural resource.)

LOOKING UPWARD

(10 minutes)

You've seen that the believer's presence and prayers comprise two of God's resources for reaching the lost. To start the process, develop a "Ten Most Wanted List" (TMWL)—listing up to ten unbelievers whom you would like to see come to Christ. Don't worry if you can't think of ten immediately. God will bring the rest to mind over the coming weeks.

10. On your own, fill out your TMWL.

If you know a lot of unbelievers, how do you decide whom to put on your TMWL? See 2 Corinthians 3:1-5. Whose names are written on your heart? Ask God to write a few names on your heart.

Ten Most Wanted

1.

2.

3.

4.

5.

6.

7.

8.

9.

10.

❏ I will faithfully pray for the salvation of the above and will attempt to reach them for Christ through personal witness.

---

11. Pair up with someone in your group (not the person you were with last session). Don't spend time telling your partner who all of your "most wanted" people are, but you may include any necessary information in your prayer. Take turns asking God to start working in one of your friends' lives. Just go down your lists: your #1, your partner's #1, your #2, and so on.

   Use the scriptures in this session as ideas for what to ask. For example, "Lord, please start convicting Gerry about his sin and your righteousness." (Can you pray that without feeling judgmental or guilty?) Or, "Lord, please free Linda from the dominion of darkness." Don't get caught up in saying something different about each person.

Afterward, pray for your partner. Ask God to give your partner the courage and wisdom and power of the Holy Spirit to be a light in his or her world this week. Ask God to start clearing away the obstacles in your partner's life that might hinder him or her from reaching out. Ask God to let you be part of this process!

ACTION STEPS

Pray. Pray daily for the people on your TMWL. (You might post the list in a prominent location in your home, business, or car as a reminder.)

Watch and listen. Be alert for the signs of spiritual blindness, poverty, and bondage in the unbelievers around you. Ask God to give you His heart of compassion for them. Ask Him to show them to you through His eyes. Keep track of your observations and come to your next session prepared to discuss them.

Reflect. How would you define the word *evangelism*? Write out your definition and be ready to share it with your group in session 3.

Read. In preparation for session 3, read the article below on proclamation and affirmation.

MINI BIBLE STUDY

(Optional)
During the coming week, read through Paul's letter to the Philippians (it's not very long). As you read, look for how Paul tells this group of believers to go about "contending . . . for the faith of the gospel" (Philippians 1:27). In other words, what strategy for reaching the lost does he teach them to use?

SHOWING AND TELLING

Telling the Truth

Repeatedly in the book of Acts, a believer stands up in a public place, proclaims the basic truths of the gospel, and up to five thousand people accept Christ. The same thing happens today in evangelistic crusades. It even happens one-on-one in chance encounters on airplanes and in college dormitories.

Telling the gospel message is essential. But often it doesn't work the way we just described. Sometimes when we tell our coworkers about Jesus, they stare at us blankly and warn the boss that we're religious fanatics. We get the treatment Paul got in Athens (Acts 11): ridicule and a cold shoulder.

Does that mean we should write our coworkers off as children of darkness? No. There is a whole other aspect of reaching the lost. We can call it *affirming* or *showing* the gospel. It is the process of being living proof of the biblical message. We affirm or demonstrate the truth of Christ by our lives.

Telling works among the *prepared*. In Acts 2, the Jews and converts to Judaism have been prepared by the whole of Old Testament history: They know about the true God's character, His justice, His promise of a Deliverer. In Acts 8, the eunuch has been involved with Judaism. In Acts 10, Cornelius has believed in the true God for some time. And in Acts 16, the Philippian jailer is prepared by a miraculous encounter with God's power. But in Athens, Paul is up against people with no preparation to understand the gospel, so his message falls flat.

Showing the Truth
Showing is how people get prepared for telling. God can prepare a heart through special circumstances or even miracles, as with the Philippian jailer. But most often God chooses to use ordinary relationships and experiences. He uses His people.

God raised up Israel to be a light to the nations (Exodus 19:6, Deuteronomy 4:5-8, Joshua 4:24, Isaiah 41:12). The idea was that when the surrounding nations saw how just and pleasant a society Israel was, they would be attracted to the God who set up that society. But Israel failed to be light, lapsing into the immoral ways of their neighbors. After God disciplined them for immorality, they failed again to be light because they turned their liberating laws into harsh, hypocritical legalism. Then the Father sent Jesus to be the true Light, to demonstrate how a person of God would really live. And when Jesus left the earth, He passed His commission on to His team: "You are the light of the world. . . . Let your light so shine before men that they may see your good deeds and glorify your Father in heaven" (Matthew 5:14,16).

That's affirmation: being living proof that the Father really is who He says He is, that Jesus really is the Son who frees people from slavery to self, that the Holy Spirit really can transform a life. This kind of showing is not a substitute for telling; if we never explain the gospel in words, people will never understand it enough to submit to Christ. But showing is an essential preparation for telling. People will buy our words when our actions back them up.

How can we grow in being living proof? There are no shortcuts. We need to contemplate the great truths of the gospel—how utterly the Father loves us, how secure our hope for our future is—until they begin to alter us at the core. But we don't have to wait until we are great saints to be light for our friends. People will notice even the small, slow changes in our ability to love, to serve, to forgive others, to forgive ourselves.

For Further Reading
Jim Petersen, *Living Proof*, chapters 13, 14, 20.
Joe Aldrich, *Gentle Persuasion*, chapters 2, 4, 5.

Mini-Decisions

Many people think evangelism is telling others about Christ, and success is convincing them to pray a sinner's prayer. But drawing someone to accept Jesus as Savior and Lord is much more a process than an event. In this session we will

- show why it's crucial to view evangelism as a process rather than an event or action,
- explore the parts of this process, and
- find that coming to Christ is really a series of "mini-decisions" on the way to conversion.

WARM UP
(15 minutes)
1. Share your definitions of evangelism from session 2. Do your definitions sound more like events, actions, and projects? Or more like processes?

2. Think of a person on your Ten Most Wanted List (TMWL, page 22). Where would you place that person on the scale below? (Substitute your name for "messenger.")

   -12 Going his or her own way
   -11 Aware of messenger
   -10 Has positive attitude toward messenger
   - 9 Aware of difference in messenger
   - 8 First aware of Bible's relevance to life
   - 7 Has positive attitude toward Bible
   - 6 Aware of basics of the gospel
   - 5 Understands meaning and implications of gospel
   - 4 Has positive attitude toward gospel
   - 3 Recognizes personal need
   - 2 Decides to act
   - 1 Repents and believes

3. a. What signs of spiritual blindness and bondage have you observed in unbelievers since session 2? Give some examples.

   b. *(Optional)* What did you learn from the mini-Bible study in session 2?

VIDEO

(20 minutes)

Bill and Gerry have known each other for several months now. But in this segment, Bill hits a brick wall when he tries to share his faith with Gerry, and later he learns why. As you watch the story unfold, think about these questions:

> **Some people are eager to discuss the gospel, while many others are indifferent or even openly hostile. What accounts for this variety, and how should you respond to it?**

TURN ON VIDEO

YOUR NOTES FROM THE VIDEO

The Holy Spirit convicts of sin, righteousness, and judgment. What a relief to discover that this responsibility has been assigned to Him, rather than to us!
(Jim Petersen, *Living Proof*)

How do you remove the obstacles between your friend and the Cross?

A FOUR-PHASE PROCESS OF LIFESTYLE EVANGELISM: MARK 4:1-20

PHASE	I. Cultivation	II. Sowing	III. Harvesting	IV. Multiplication
Picture	The Soil = Human Hearts	The Seed = Gospel Truth	The Grain = Reproduced Life of Jesus Christ	Crop = Christian Community
Explanation	Speaks to the **heart** through relationship. Focus on caring.	Speaks to the **mind** through revelation. Focus on communication.	Speaks to the **will** for a faith response. Focus on conversion.	Speaks to the **whole man** for growth and going! Focus on completion (Colossians 1:28).
Emphasis	The **presence** of the believer. Building a friendship bridge.	**Presentation** of the gospel. Giving understanding of truth.	**Persuasion.** Encouraging a meaningful decision of faith.	**Participation.** Integration into Body.
Obstacles	Indifference / Antagonism	Ignorance / Error	Indecision / Love of darkness	Isolation / Inward focus
Some Examples	Nicodemus—John 3 / Woman at well—John 4	Ethiopian eunuch—Acts 8 / Woman at well—John 4	Philippian jailer—Acts 16 / Woman at well—John 4	Jerusalem converts—Acts 2:40-41 / Samaritan awakening—Acts 8

Mini-Decisions
Some of the specific "mini-decisions" that could be made in each phase.

I. Cultivation
–12	Going his or her own way
–11	Aware of messenger
–10	Has positive attitude toward messenger
–9	Aware of difference in messenger
–8	First aware of Bible's relevance to life

II. Sowing
–7	Has positive attitude toward Bible
–6	Aware of basics of the gospel
–5	Understands meaning and implications of gospel
–4	Has positive attitude toward gospel

III. Harvesting
–3	Recognizes personal need
–2	Decides to act
–1	Repents and believes
★	New creature in Christ

IV. Multiplication
+1	Faith confirmation and grounding
+2	Assimilation into a caring community
+3	Growing and maturing into Christlikeness
+4	Going! Mobilization to reproduce

Why does the direct approach often fail?

FOUR SOILS
In Matthew 13:1-23, Jesus tells a parable about seed sown in four kinds of soil. The seed is the same in each case, but its fruitfulness depends on the readiness of the soil.

The seed, says Jesus, is the Word of God. When sown in packed, rocky, or thorn-infested soil, it fails to produce a crop. Only clean, well-tilled soil is fruitful. It seems that before we sow the Word, we need to break up the unplowed ground, dig out the rocks, and uproot the thorns. If the soil is a human heart, then we need to cultivate that heart, clearing out obstacles and preparing it to receive the Word. This is cultivation.

Only when cultivation is well underway do we sow the Word, continuing our cultivating all along. When the Word produces spiritual birth in the person's heart, we can harvest that crop—a new believer. But we don't just hide that harvest in a barn; we equip and send the new believer to multiply, bearing fruit in others' lives.

For a fanatic, he [Bill] is a pretty decent guy. (Gerry)

REFLECTING ON THE VIDEO

(30 minutes)

4. Some people are eager to discuss the gospel, while many others are indifferent or even openly hostile.

   a. What accounts for this variety?

   b. How should you respond to it?

Bill and his group have discovered that evangelism is a process. We might define evangelism as follows.

Success in Evangelism
Taking the initiative, in the power of the Holy Spirit, to help a person move one step closer in the process of coming to Christ.

---

5. How does this definition compare to the ones you offered in question 1?

6. Steve used restaurant tableware to illustrate the process of mini-decisions. Look at the list of mini-decisions on page 27. If you filled in "Bill" where it says "the messenger," where would you put Gerry on this scale?

CONVERSION

THE CHRISTIAN ⟶
THE HOLY SPIRIT ⟶
THE WORD OF GOD ⟶

7. a. What are some of the obstacles between Gerry and a decision for Christ?

b. What are some obstacles faced by unbelievers you know?

8. Having placed Gerry on the mini-decision scale, why do you think he rejected Bill's invitation to see a musical at church?

9. How does the list of mini-decisions square with your own experience of coming to Christ? What mini-decisions did you make along the way? What influences did God use to clear away the obstacles?

LOOKING UPWARD

(10 minutes)
Divide into pairs.

10. Choose one person from your TMWL. Tell your partner what phase of the evangelism process (cultivation, sowing, etc.) you think this person is in. Also, explain briefly why you selected that stage.

11. What mini-decision is next in the process for this person?

12. What do you think needs to happen to encourage that mini-decision?

13. a. Pray for your partner, asking God to grant the insight and compassion your partner needs to cultivate a friendship with an unbeliever. Ask God to give your partner discernment about how to relate to that unbeliever and to provide the time and energy the relationship needs.

b. Finally, pray for each of the people on your TMWL. Ask God to work in their lives and reveal His love through you and any other ways.

ACTION STEPS

Pray. Pray daily for the people on your TMWL. Here are some ideas for prayer.

Conversion is a process. . . . Every time a person confronts an obstacle, it's decision time. Few of us make it in one big decision. Instead, it's a multitude of small choices—mini-decisions that a person makes toward Christ.

Defining evangelism as we have introduces the "time factor." According to the diagram below, where should we be investing our time? What are the implications for your schedule if you accept this model?

The RIGHT "TRY-Angle"

The WRONG "TRY-Angle"

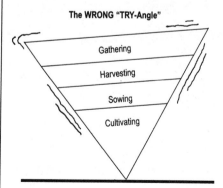

Spend most of your time cultivating, and don't stop when you start sowing. If you neglect cultivating, you may never get to the harvest.

Pray for Unbelievers

1. That God draws them to Himself (John 6:44).
2. That they seek to know God (Deuteronomy 4:29, Acts 17:27).
3. That they believe the Scriptures (Romans 10:17, 1 Thessalonians 2:13).
4. That Satan is bound from blinding them to the truth (Matthew 13:19, 2 Corinthians 4:4).
5. That the Holy Spirit works in them (John 16:8-13).
6. That God sends someone to lead them to Christ (Matthew 9:37-38).
7. That they believe in Christ as Savior (John 1:12, 5:24).
8. That they turn from sin (Acts 3:19, 17:30-31).
9. That they confess Christ as Lord (Romans 10:9-10).
10. That they yield all to follow Christ (2 Corinthians 5:15, Philippians 3:7-8).
11. That they take root and grow in Christ (Colossians 2:6-7).

Assess. Where do you think each of the people on your TMWL currently sits in the scale on page 27? Write their names next to the appropriate place on the scale. Write in pencil so that you can move the names later.

MINI BIBLE STUDY

1. Read Matthew 5:46-47, 9:9-13 (see page 35), and 11:19.

   a. What was Jesus' attitude toward tax collectors and sinners, and why?

   b. What are some of the potential risks of socializing with sinners?

   c. What are some of the potential benefits?

> "If you love those who love you, what reward will you get? Are not even the tax collectors doing that? And if you greet only your brothers, what are you doing more than others? Do not even pagans do that?"
>
> (Matthew 5:46-47)

> "The Son of Man came eating and drinking, and they say, 'Here is a glutton and a drunkard, a friend of tax collectors and "sinners."' But wisdom is proved right by her actions."
>
> (Matthew 11:19)

Note: Tax collectors were Jews who worked for the hated Romans. Rome set a total amount of taxes it expected from an area, and the collector's job was to obtain at least that much. If he fell short of his quota, the deficit came out of his own pocket. But whatever extra he could collect he kept. Most tax collectors used extortion and deceit to make their living, often with the help of a Roman soldier or two for muscle. Because they collaborated with Rome, exploited fellow Jews, and associated with defiled Gentiles, tax collectors were regarded as scum by good Jews. They were generally rowdy and immoral, and they tended to consort with people of like character. A modern parallel might be loan sharks.

For Further Reading
Jim Petersen, *Living Proof,* chapters 16, 19.
Joe Aldrich, *Life-Style Evangelism,* chapter 4.
Joe Aldrich, *Gentle Persuasion,* chapters 1-2.
Richard Peace, *Small Group Evangelism,* chapter 2.

Finding Common Ground

A blind person in prison can hardly be expected to initiate a friendship that will lead toward Christ. It's up to us to make the first move. In this session we'll

- start learning how to cultivate by *taking the initiative* and *developing common ground* with unbelievers,
- look at reasons why we resist making friends with unbelievers, and
- explore ways to overcome those barriers.

WARM UP
(10 minutes)

1. a. Do most of the people on your TMWL (Ten Most Wanted List) fall in the cultivating, sowing, or harvesting section of the chart on page 27?

   b. How should this affect the way you relate to them?

2. Think of someone you consider to be a good friend. Other than Christ, what do you have in common? (Consider your interests, concerns, experiences, and the way you think.)

VIDEO
(20 minutes)

This time our group members learn how to establish *common ground* between themselves and the nonChristians in their world. They also have to face some reasons why making friends and finding common ground with unbelievers can be a challenge. As you watch this segment, consider the following:

What keeps believers and unbelievers apart? What brings them together?

"It is not the healthy who need a doctor, but the sick. I have not come to call the righteous, but sinners to repentance."
(Luke 5:31-32)

Frequently the unsaved are viewed as enemies rather than victims of the Enemy. Spirituality is viewed as separation from the unsaved. The new Christian is told he has "nothing in common" with his unsaved associates. Quite frankly, I have a lot in common with them: a mortgage, car payments, kids who misbehave, a lawn to mow, a car to wash, a less-than-perfect marriage, a few too many pounds around my waist, and an interest in sports, hobbies, and other activities they enjoy. It is well to remember that Jesus was called "a friend of sinners." A *friend of sinners.*
(Joe Aldrich, *Life-Style Evangelism*)

TURN ON VIDEO

FROM THE VIDEO

Sources of Common Ground Between Believers and Unbelievers
- Chance experiences that touch our common humanity
- Hobbies and interests, like fishing
- Helping out with a skill you happen to have
- Welcoming people into your home
- Drawing people out with questions about themselves

Risks of Reaching Out
- Rejection
- Failure
- Contamination

REFLECTING
ON THE VIDEO
(30 minutes)

3. What keeps believers and unbelievers apart?

Believers' Attitudes

Unbelievers' Attitudes

Our ministry is to the dead. . . . But death is repulsive. It is ugly. . . . So it is with the spiritually dead. Their behavior is often ugly and embarrassing to us. We feel offended by the things they do and say. We're anxious to get them converted so that they can clean up their act. But the world is not a nice place to live in, and often the people of the world are neither respectable nor nice to be around. Nevertheless, it is precisely to these people that we are sent.

(Jim Petersen, *Living Proof*)

What keeps us from connecting with unbelievers?

4. Despite these barriers, how is it possible for us to make real friendships with unbelievers?

5. *(Optional)* Describe a time when someone created some common ground with you by serving you or being a friend.

6. a. In Matthew 9:10-13, how did Jesus go about establishing common ground with sinners?

   b. What risks was He taking in doing this?

While Jesus was having dinner at Matthew's house, many tax collectors and "sinners" came and ate with him and his disciples. When the Pharisees saw this, they asked his disciples, "Why does your teacher eat with tax collectors and 'sinners'?"

On hearing this, Jesus said, "It is not the healthy who need a doctor, but the sick. But go and learn what this means: 'I desire mercy, not sacrifice.' For I have not come to call the righteous, but sinners."
(Matthew 9:10-13)

What brings us together?

Most of us fear that who we are inside just isn't enough. So we cover up our honest questions and doubts thinking we won't sound spiritual. But in doing this we forfeit our most important asset in evangelism—our real person. Not to accept our humanness means we lose our point of authentic contact with the world. . . . When we get a good look at Jesus we will see that it is not our humanity we need to fear.

(Rebecca Pippert,
*Out of the Saltshaker
and into the World*)

7. a. What do you think Jesus would have done in Jackie's situation at her party?

   b. What would you do, and why?

8. In sessions 5 and 6 you will discuss ways to handle situations like Jackie's party and Matthew's dinner. How do you feel right now about going into situations like these for the sake of reaching sinners?

Jackie resisted a friendship with her neighbors because she feared *contamination* of her children, her home, and herself. But others of us are more afraid of *rejection* or *failure*.

9. a. How do you feel when you make a friendly overture toward someone and the door is slammed in your face?

   b. How can a relationship with Christ and a group of supportive believers enable you to bounce back from that kind of rejection and try again?

   c. How do you think God views people who do their best to build a friendship and pray for their friend but fail to win the trust they need to take the next step?

LOOKING UPWARD

(20 minutes)

10. a. (If your group numbers five of more, break up into pairs or triplets.) Select one person from your TMWL with whom you might like to build a relationship. Then take a few minutes to ask God how you can establish common ground with that person. Tell Him the ideas you have. If you don't have any ideas, tell Him you'll make yourself available and trust Him to guide the conversation.

    b. How could you go about establishing common ground with the person you chose? (For some ideas, see the box on page 34 and the article on pages 37-39.)

c. Plan with your partners how to make yourself available to build common ground with the person you chose. You could invite him or her for a meal or a sporting event. If you need to start slower, try a conversation at the office. Commit yourself to spending at least half an hour this week with the person you've selected. (If a date won't work this week, then *schedule* it this week for another week.)

d. Write down the names of the people your partners are going to meet with, and plan to pray for them this week.

ACTION STEPS

Meet with your unbelieving friend for at least half an hour. Don't worry about turning the conversation toward spiritual things; just try to get to know the person. Where is she from? What does he like? What's on her mind? What is he interested in? Don't be afraid to ask questions; people love to talk about themselves.

Pray for your partners who are also meeting with their unbelieving friends. Also, pray at least once this week for the people on your TMWL, especially for the person with whom you are meeting.

MINI BIBLE STUDY
(Optional)

1. a. Read Matthew 5:14-16. What does Jesus say it takes to be a good testimony for Christ to an unbeliever?

   b. In practical terms, what do you think it means to be "the light of the world" and to "let your light shine before men"?

2. a. What attitudes and actions make for a poor testimony (Matthew 6:1-6, 16-18)?

   b. Why do you think it's a poor testimony to practice your "acts of righteousness" in front of people?

3. How is it possible to let your light shine before people without doing acts of righteousness before them?

FRIENDSHIP 101

If you ask believers why they aren't building friendships with the unbelievers at their workplaces, in their neighborhoods, or among the parents of their kids' friends, they will often reply, "I've tried, but we have nothing in common." And it often seems true. Believers are interested in spiritual matters or issues at church, while unbelievers may be indifferent to anything of eternal significance. The topics that interest nonChristians may seem shallow to those of us with a deeper perspective.

"You are the light of the world. A city on a hill cannot be hidden. Neither do people light a lamp and put it under a bowl. Instead they put it on its stand, and it gives light to everyone in the house. In the same way, let your light shine before men, that they may see your good deeds and praise your Father in heaven."
(Matthew 5:14-16)

"Be careful not to do your 'acts of righteousness' before men, to be seen by them. If you do, you will have no reward from your Father in heaven.

"So when you give to the needy, do not announce it with trumpets, as the hypocrites do in the synagogues and on the streets, to be honored by men. I tell you the truth, they have received their reward in full. But when you give to the needy, do not let your left hand know what your right hand is doing, so that your giving may be in secret. Then your Father, who sees what is done in secret, will reward you.

"And when you pray, do not be like the hypocrites, for they love to pray standing in the synagogues and on the street corners to be seen by men. I tell you the truth, they have received their reward in full. But when you pray, go into your room, close the door and pray to your Father, who is unseen. Then your Father, who sees what is done in secret, will reward you. . . .

"When you fast, do not look somber as the hypocrites do, for they disfigure their faces to show men they are fasting. I tell you the truth, they have received their reward in full. But when you fast, put oil on your head and wash your face, so that it will not be obvious to men that you are fasting, but only to your Father, who is unseen; and your Father, who sees what is done in secret, will reward you."
(Matthew 6:1-6,16-18)

Family

However, the fact is that we have a lot of things in common with unbelievers in our world. Children, for instance. There is bound to be someone around with children the same ages as yours. If your children are grown, maybe you know a younger couple who would appreciate your taking an interest in their child-rearing blues. If you've never had children, are there other couples or singles who share your adults-only lifestyle? Or parents who would revel in a baby-sitting aunt or uncle?

Work

If you are a professional, you might make connections with others in your profession; someone in your field might leap at a support group or a one-on-one friendship to talk shop and share frustrations. If you're a secretary, seek out other secretaries in your building for lunch or after-work aerobics. If you're a mechanic, seek mechanics. There's no law that says lawyers and mechanics can't be great friends, but if you're afraid of having nothing in common, look for people who are guaranteed to share similar interests. You might be surprised at how receptive a near-stranger will be if you just call and say, "I don't have any friends who are hairdressers like me, and I want to hear how you run your shop. Can we get together?"

If you work with someone, you have something ready-made in common. It's sad that so often workplace socializing stays on a surface level. Christians need to develop the art of drawing people out. You may feel afraid of grilling people with questions about themselves; it seems nosy. But most people enjoy talking about themselves, their families, where they grew up, where they've lived, and so on. Past history is usually a safe subject and can lead to surprising connections: "You used to love fishing? Wow, so did I! Let's. . . ."

The Art of Friendship

Making friends is an art. Some of us are more gifted than others. But with the Holy Spirit's help, all of us can take some steps. Here are four stages of building a friendship, along with some of the elements of each stage. You don't have to become expert at all of them right away, but this will get you started.

1. ***Taking the initiative.***

   • Being the first to say hello.
   • Being friendly.
   • Making small talk.
   • Remembering the other person's name and using it often.
   • Being genuinely interested in him or her.

2. ***Establishing rapport.*** Rapport is an attitude of mutual acceptance.

   • Thinking in your heart, "I accept you as you are."
   • Listening with interest to what the other person says.
   • Expressing approval; giving compliments where they are due.
   • Being sensitive to specific needs and opportunities where you could serve.
   • Looking for an occasion to invite the other person to join you in some activity.

3. ***Being a friend.*** Friendship has a price tag: time. It means putting other people first.

• Listening; being attentive to thoughts and feelings.
• Affirming the other person; expressing what you like about him or her.
• Being transparent; openly expressing your own feelings.
• Letting your friend serve you and do you favors.
• Accepting your friend as he or she is, without trying to reform him or her.

4. *Building a relationship.*

• Letting the other person know what you're thinking; allowing that person to see inside you.
• Seeking the other person's counsel.
• Sharing your personal resources: money, abilities, and so on.
• Making time for him or her.
• Not overdoing it; not trying to control the other person or be possessive.

For Further Reading
Jim Petersen, *Living Proof*, chapters 5, 6, 12, 17.
Joe Aldrich, *Life-Style Evangelism*, chapters 3, 10.
Joe Aldrich, *Gentle Persuasion*, chapters 6-8.
Richard Peace, *Small Group Evangelism*, chapter 3.
Rebecca Pippert, *Out of the Saltshaker and into the World*, chapters 6-8.

Being a Good Testimony

Jesus said, "You are the light of the world." That's great, but how? In this session, we will

- explore what being a good testimony *is* and *isn't*,
- see how to be a good testimony when asked to participate in an activity we think is wrong,
- learn the first step in articulating our biblical worldview: "raising the flag," and
- begin practicing the next step: learning what nonChristians believe.

WARM UP

(15 minutes)

1. What happened when you spent time with unbelievers this week? Talk about the common ground you did or didn't find.

2. Describe a situation you could get into with an unbeliever that would make you say, "See, I knew this would happen if I spent time with pagans!"

3. a. In the first paragraph of 1 Corinthians 9:19-27 (right margin), how does Paul say he makes his life a good testimony to unbelievers?

   b. Does this mean he's free to do whatever he wants? How does the rest of the passage apply?

Though I am free and belong to no man, I make myself a slave to everyone, to win as many as possible. To the Jews I became like a Jew, to win the Jews. To those under the law I became like one under the law (though I myself am not under the law), so as to win those under the law. To those not having the law I became like one not having the law (though I am not free from God's law but am under Christ's law), so as to win those not having the law. To the weak I became weak, to win the weak. I have become all things to all men so that by all possible means I might save some. I do all this for the sake of the gospel, that I may share in its blessings.

Do you not know that in a race all the runners run, but only one gets the prize? Run in such a way as to get the prize. Everyone who competes in the games goes into strict training. They do it to get a crown that will not last; but we do it to get a crown that will last forever. Therefore I do not run like a man running aimlessly; I do not fight like a man beating the air. No, I beat my body and make it my slave so that after I have preached to others, I myself will not be disqualified for the prize.

(1 Corinthians 9:19-27)

Evangelism is a way of living beautifully and then opening up those webs of relationship to the nonChristian.

(Joe Aldrich)

The best argument for Christianity is Christians; their joy, their certainty, their completeness. But the strongest argument against Christianity is also Christians—when they are sombre and joyless, when they are self-righteous and smug in complacent consecration, when they are narrow and repressive, then Christianity dies a thousand deaths.

(Sheldon Vanauken, *A Severe Mercy*)

Live such good lives among the pagans that, though they accuse you of doing wrong, they may see your good deeds and glorify God on the day he visits us.

(1 Peter 2:12)

(20 minutes)
In this segment our group discovers that many of their values are based on things other than the Bible, and Bill and Jackie get to apply the lesson to an evening out with Gerry and Linda. As you watch this segment, ask yourself,

How do Bill and Jackie demonstrate a good testimony here?

TURN ON VIDEO

Being a Good Testimony
• is *being light in a dark world by living with grace (unconditional, forgiving love) and truth,*
• is not *flaunting our moral righteousness.*

Grace. We can learn to live among people with very different values without making them feel judged. We can maintain our good testimony when asked to participate in an activity we believe is wrong by

- expressing our personal choice simply and without explanation (and perhaps suggesting an alternative);
- not using our faith as an explanation for abstaining; and
- not imposing our choice on the unbeliever.

Truth. We can help an unbeliever move from –10 to –8 on our decision scale (page 27). We begin by "raising our flag"—identifying ourselves not as someone who abstains from things but *as someone who gets a lot of great ideas from the Bible.* That's a productive testimony.

THE BALANCED COMMUNICATOR

Christ's love compels us, because we are convinced that one died for all.
(2 Corinthians 5:14)

HOLY HUDDLE

LEGALISM

HARDENING OF THE CATEGORIES

CEMENT

CASE I.
THE SPIRITUAL PORCUPINE
• Loses his audience
• No longer salt and light

ACCEPTANCE

ASSIMILATION

CASE II.
THE SPIRITUAL CHAMELEON
• Loses his message
• No longer salt and light

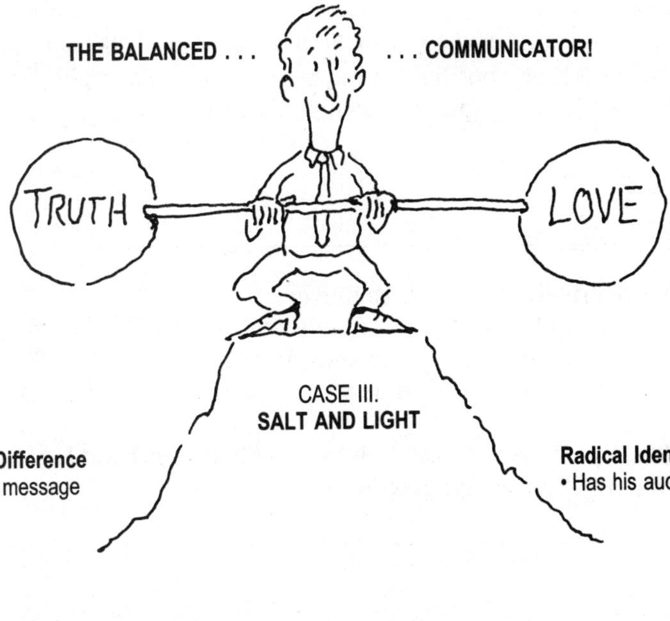

THE BALANCED . . . . . . COMMUNICATOR!

TRUTH

LOVE

CASE III.
SALT AND LIGHT

Radical Difference
• Has his message

Radical Identification
• Has his audience

REFLECTING
ON THE VIDEO

(35 minutes)

4. How did Bill and Jackie demonstrate a good testimony in this segment? That is,

   a. How did they keep from connecting faith in Christ with moral righteousness?

   b. How did they identify themselves as people who get valuable insights from the Bible?

5. What would you have done differently in their situation? Why?

6. Why is it crucial to avoid connecting faith in Christ with abstaining from certain popular activities?

7. What worth can you see in identifying ourselves as "people who get valuable insights from the Bible" rather than as "Christians" or as "members of such-and-such church"?

8. *(Optional)* Compare Matthew 5:14-16 to Matthew 6:1. What is the difference between letting your light shine before others and highlighting your "acts of righteousness" (prayer, fasting, giving)?

Saying no gracefully.

Function Effectively Among Unbelievers
1. Know what God's Word says about moral standards.
2. Know what you personally can and can't handle.
3. Based on these facts, determine what your personal standards really are.
4. Challenge your comfort zone, but stay within your boundaries.
5. Develop a way to say no gracefully.

This session deals with principle number 5, "Develop a way to say no gracefully." Session 6 will address the others.

9. Divide into pairs. In the following scenarios, one of you will play the role of a believer, and the other will play an unbeliever. The believer will practice saying no gracefully. Then switch roles. After both have tried saying no, discuss what you think you did well or poorly, and how you could improve.

- The unbeliever invites the believer and spouse to join the nonChristian couple in their hot tub.
- The unbeliever offers the believer cocaine.
- The unbeliever invites the believer to a seance.

10. Regather as a large group. What did you learn from this exercise? How did it feel? Where do you still want improvement or clearer understanding?

11. The action steps for the next three sessions will help you learn to express a biblical outlook as part of an ordinary conversation. Right now, how do you feel about your ability to do this?

1	2	3	4	5	6	7	8	9	10
VERY CONFIDENT									NOT AT ALL CONFIDENT

12. Go over the action steps below. Choose an issue to focus on, and pair up with a partner.

LOOKING UPWARD

(5 minutes)

13. Close in prayer with your partner. Ask the Lord to show you His views on the issue you have chosen, and also to teach you how the unbelievers around you view this same issue. Ask Him to help you live in the light of His outlook while loving those who don't. Pray for discernment and compassion. Choose one or two people on your TMWLs to pray for in particular.

ACTION STEPS

Learn. For the next three sessions, your action steps will help you learn to discuss important issues biblically with secular people. Your objectives are as follows:

1. To become more sensitive to the receiver of the message by seeking to *understand how people think and why.*
2. To become confident and skilled in relating to unbelievers by learning to *ask relevant questions and listen actively.*
3. To learn how to convey biblical perspectives in secular language, in order to spark the unbeliever's interest in spiritual discussions.

LIVING THE TRUTH

One way we live as light is by showing how our worldview affects our values, our behavior, and ultimately our joy and peace (1 Peter 3:15). We must learn to articulate our values in secular jargon so that we can discuss them in natural conversations with unbelievers. We also need to learn the secular world's views and vocabulary on these same key issues, so that we can discuss them in ways that unbelievers will find intelligible and thought provoking. The fourth mini-decision listed on page 27 is becoming aware that we are different. Conversations about important issues are meant to demonstrate that we *are* different before we even start talking about Christ.

To have effective conversations about values, we need to

- know what the Bible says about major life issues;
- live what the Bible says about major life issues (our words will be hypocrisy rather than light if we don't practice what we say);
- articulate in secular language what the Bible says about major life issues; and
- listen and discern where the other person is regarding a given issue.

The action projects for the next several sessions will help develop these skills.

Here is what you need to do before you meet for session 6:

1. Choose one of the following issues to focus on.

    • Success
    • Work and leisure
    • Children
    • Relationships with the opposite sex
    • Money and self-identity
    • Absolutes/right and wrong

2. Pair up with a partner to explore an issue.
3. Read at least one *secular* magazine article or one book chapter about that issue (more if you can).
4. Study what the Bible says about the issue, and develop your own "opinion" from a biblical perspective. You can study on your own or meet with your partner to study. (On pages 46-47 are biblical passages to get you started on this Bible study. If you like, you can use a concordance, a topical Bible, or other reference books for further study.) Write down what you learn about your issue.

Pray. Also, keep praying for the people on your TMWL. Look for ways to let your light shine with gracious love before them.

BIBLE STUDY

You'll be using these Bible studies for sessions 5 and 6. Each week, choose a reasonable number of passages and questions for yourself. Try to ask yourself all of the questions under your issue for at least *one or two* passages per week.

Success. *The American Heritage Dictionary* defines success as "the achievement of something desired, planned, or attempted." In the following passages, examine what God has desired and planned for men and women.

    • What is a successful human from God's point of view?
    • How important is it to God that people become financially or professionally successful? Why?

See, for example, Matthew 5:1-12, 25:14-30, 28:16-20; Luke 6:20-26, 9:22-26, 12:16-21, 18:18-30; John 15:12-17; Romans 8:29; and 1 Corinthians 9:24-27. If you have more time, look at Ecclesiastes 1:12–2:26, 5:10–6:12, 12:13-14.

Work and leisure. In the following passages, look for

    • the origin of work,
    • the purpose of work before and after the Fall of man,
    • how God views work,
    • the purpose of rest, and
    • the balance between work and rest.

See Genesis 1:26-30, 2:4-24, 3:17-19; Exodus 18:13-26, 20:8-11; Deuteronomy 8:17-18; Proverbs 6:6-11, 22:9; Ecclesiastes 2:17-26, 5:18-20; Matthew 11:28-29; and 2 Thessalonians 3:6-15.

Children.

• How important to God are children?
• What insights does the Bible offer regarding the raising of children?
• How does parental character affect children?

See Genesis 1:28; Exodus 20:5-6; Psalm 127:3; Proverbs 13:24, 19:18, 22:6, 29:15; Matthew 7:9, 10:37, 18:1-6; 2 Corinthians 12:14; and Ephesians 6:1-4. The successes and failures of Abraham, Issac, and Jacob as fathers in Genesis 12–50 are also instructive. Notice the traits that pass through the generations, and the good and bad things the men and their wives do in raising their children.

Relationships with the opposite sex.

• Why did God make two sexes?
• Why did He institute marriage?
• What makes a marriage work?
• How does God view extramarital sex?
• How should spouses relate to each other?
• In Ephesians 5:21-33, why does God emphasize respect toward husbands and sacrificial love toward wives?

See Genesis 1:26-27, 2:4–3:24; Proverbs 5:15-20, 20:6, 31:10-31; 1 Corinthians 7:1-40; Ephesians 5:21-33; and Hebrews 13:4. You might also find the Song of Songs interesting.

Money and self-identity.

• Why did God create money and material things?
• Is money evil?
• Does God love poor people more than rich ones, or vice versa?
• Is wealth a sign that God is pleased with you?
• Is poverty a sign of lack of faith?
• Is poverty proof of humility?
• How does God want people to regard and treat their possessions?
• Should money affect the way you feel about yourself?
• Who owns what you possess?

See Psalm 50:10-12; Haggai 2:8; Matthew 6:19-34; Luke 6:20-26, 12:13-34, 16:1-15, 18:18-30; 2 Corinthians 4:18, 8:1–9:15; and 1 Timothy 6:17-19.

Absolutes/right and wrong.

• By what standard(s) can we determine what is right and wrong? (See Exodus 20:1-17; Psalm 19:7-14; Matthew 4:4, 23:34-40; John 15:9-17; Romans 13:8-10; 2 Timothy 3:16-17; and James 1:5-8.)
• Do all people have an inner sense of right and wrong? What difference does it make? (See Romans 1:18-32.)

Ninety percent of evangelism is love.
(Bob Smith)

THE EXAMPLE OF SERGIO
The week [Sergio] graduated, he came to me and announced he had made two decisions. He had decided to put God first, and to be honest. With that he moved back to his hometown, rented an office, and opened his own law practice.

A few months later, one of the local farmers was on the verge of losing his farm because of unpaid back taxes. The farm went up for public auction, and Sergio bought it. A murmur ran through the town, for the purchase appeared to be typical of the opportunism that characterized the rest of Sergio's family. But what Sergio did next stopped the town in its tracks. He went to the farmer and gave him back the deed to his property, instructing him to repay the debt when he was able!

Sergio didn't have to do this. It was his legal right to keep the farm. But he acted with grace, not merely with justice—just as God does with us.

Sergio probably has another thirty-five years in business ahead of him. If he continues the way he has begun, the sheer influence of his life will go a long way toward breaking up the spiritual soil in that valley where he lives.
(Jim Petersen, *Living Proof*)

WHAT MAKES A CHRISTIAN DIFFERENT?

A person who lives in faith, hope, love, and truth sows life in all of his or her relationships. That person is the light of the world.

Faith. Believers are betting their lives that Jesus is who He says He is and that He will keep His promises.

Hope. Believers don't need to fear the present or the future. Since Jesus was raised from death, we have confidence that we, too, will be raised to eternal life. Because He ascended to the Father and even now defends our case, we are secure in the Father's love for us. We can run to Him at any time with our needs and concerns. And because we know that Jesus will return to bring justice, we need not despair over the threat of nuclear war, oppression, or environmental calamities.

Love. We love because we are loved. We are free to love because we don't have to focus our energy on protecting ourselves from hurt or earning someone's approval.

Grace. God treats us not as we deserve, but with forgiving, patient love. That is grace. We treat others with the grace we have received when we look past a person's sins to see what God wants to do in his or her life. People aren't used to grace—they're used to either condemnation or indulgence. To be treated with grace is to taste redemption. Have you ever found yourself being accepted and understood when you expected and deserved the opposite? It's overwhelming.

Truth. The world muddles through without moral absolutes. Self-centered coping strategies keep backfiring. But the more we live by biblical truth, the more our families and work reflect a wholeness and integrity for which the world wants an explanation.

But we must be sure that the truth we're living by is God's truth, not religious tradition or the values of our culture. We must ask ourselves, "Where did I get my opinions on finances, success, marriage, child-raising, business, time-use, sex, people, pleasure, education, progress, society, sports, politics, and religion?" It will take some work to find out what the Bible says about all of these issues, but the work is infinitely worthwhile. And once we can trace our values back to God's Word, communicating our faith becomes vastly easier. We can discuss any subject and the conversation will naturally turn to the good news.

Hope is attractive because it produces joy, peace, self-control, and endurance. Love and grace are what all people thirst for. And the stable life that comes from living by truth is a powerful testimony to the truth of our faith.

Do we fall short? Of course. But if we are truly pursuing God, meditating on the shocking truths of the gospel, our life will be transformed more and more into this pattern.

For Further Reading
Jim Petersen, *Living Proof*, chapters 9-11.
Joe Aldrich, *Life-Style Evangelism*, chapter 1.
Joe Aldrich, *Gentle Persuasion*, chapter 3.

Can We Please Everyone?

We've seen that to be effective among unbelievers, we have to know how to say no gracefully to activities we think are wrong. But how do we decide what's right and what's wrong? And what do we do about the other believers who are watching our activities with pagans? In this session we will

- identify the desire to fit into Christian culture as one of the main reasons we resist involvement with unbelievers;
- come to personal convictions, based on the Bible, for our lifestyle;
- learn how to live out those convictions without alienating unbelievers or sanctioning their behavior; and
- learn the next step in expressing our biblical views naturally; that is, asking questions of unbelievers.

WARM UP
(5 minutes)

1. Look down your TMWL. What is one habit of one of those people that makes it hard for you to be around that person?

VIDEO
(20 minutes)

Through encounters with unbelievers, our video group has run into a lot of ethical dilemmas. How can they love and associate with unbelievers

- who have offensive habits?
- without being drawn into their vices?
- without offending believers who have strict moral codes?
- so that they don't confuse "disputable matters" with a relationship with Christ?

As you watch the video, consider these questions:

What are disputable matters? How should I deal with them?

TURN ON VIDEO

FROM THE VIDEO

Dealing With Unbelievers Who Have Offensive Habits
1. *Let the Holy Spirit clean up the unbeliever's act.* It's His job to handle the damage your friend will do to himself or herself and others while he or she is moving toward the Cross.
2. *Be God-pleasers, not man-pleasers.* What other people think of you is not your problem.
3. *Get God's point of view on ethical issues from the Bible.* Be sure your own choices are guided by the Bible.
4. *Learn to apply your own convictions gracefully, without alienating others.*

Accept him whose faith is weak, without passing judgment on disputable matters. One man's faith allows him to eat everything, but another man, whose faith is weak, eats only vegetables. The man who eats everything must not look down on him who does not, and the man who does not eat everything must not condemn the man who does, for God has accepted him. Who are you to judge someone else's servant? To his own master he stands or falls. And he will stand, for the Lord is able to make him stand.

(Romans 14:1-4)

ON THE VIDEO

(35 minutes)

The Bible Says There Are Three Types of Activities
• Those that are always right.
• Those that are always wrong.
• "Disputable matters" (Romans 14:1).

---

2. Define "disputable matters" in your own words? (Paul explains what he means in Romans 14.)

The Video Group Listed These Disputable Matters
• Using "profanity"
• Drinking alcohol "in moderation"
• Dancing
• What it means to be in the world but not of it
• Watching R-rated movies

You may feel that some items on this list are not disputable, that the Bible says they are clearly right or clearly wrong. That's okay; maybe the video group needs to do more Bible homework.

---

3. As a group come up with your own list of disputables. What issues are disputed among believers whom you deal with? (These would be any issues that are in fact disputed among believers, whether or not you think you have an air-tight biblical case for your view.)

The tension: Please weak Christians or appeal to the lost?

4. Here is a review from session 5. Let's say you know the amount of sex in an R-rated movie is usually enough to cause you to lust.

a. An unbeliever asks you to some particular R-rated movie. What would you say? (Let one person answer, then let the group offer feedback on how effective that answer seemed.)

b. You see another believer you know going into an R-rated movie with an unbeliever. What goes through your mind?

Hayden faced a dilemma. If he made his lifestyle appealing to unbelievers and new believers, he risked offending weak believers. But if he pleased weak believers, he risked losing his testimony to unbelievers and new believers.

5. a. Peter faced this same dilemma in Galatians 2:11-16. What did Peter decide to do?

b. What did Paul think of that decision? Why did he feel that way?

6. In light of this biblical example, what do you think Hayden should do, and why?

7. What would be easy or hard for you about doing this?

When Peter came to Antioch, I [Paul] opposed him to his face, because he was clearly in the wrong. Before certain men came from James, he used to eat with the Gentiles. But when they arrived, he began to draw back and separate himself from the Gentiles because he was afraid of those who belonged to the circumcision group. The other Jews joined him in his hypocrisy, so that by their hypocrisy even Barnabas was led astray.

When I saw that they were not acting in line with the truth of the gospel, I said to Peter in front of them all, "You are a Jew, yet you live like a Gentile and not like a Jew. How is it, then, that you force Gentiles to follow Jewish customs?

"We who are Jews by birth and not 'Gentile sinners' know that a man is not justified by observing the law, but by faith in Jesus Christ."

(Galatians 2:11-16)

The fact that some believers may safely participate in an activity does not mean that all may. It doesn't even mean you're a weakling if you can't handle something that someone else can.

The article on page 54 offers two biblical guidelines for knowing whether you should participate in a disputable matter. Studying what the Bible says is clearly right and clearly wrong, and coming to your own biblically based convictions about disputable matters, should make you vastly more comfortable as you relate to unbelievers.

It is impossible to act in such a way that we will be universally understood and accepted.

(Joe Aldrich, *Life-Style Evangelism*)

LOOKING UPWARD

(10 minutes)

8. Get together with your action-step partner. Compare notes on what you learned from reading secular literature. What did the nonChristian writers seem to believe about the issue you selected?

9. As a partnership, choose one or two questions about your issue that you would feel natural asking an unbeliever. You'll be using these questions in your action steps this week. (Use some of the questions listed below, or make up your own.)

10. Pray with your partner. Ask God to show you how to build lifestyles that have integrity and are attractive to unbelievers. Ask Him to enable you to sort through your questions about what's okay and what's not okay for you. Pray for the people on your TMWLs, using the box on page 30 as a guideline.

ACTION STEPS

Pray. Keep praying for the people on your TMWL.

Relate. Using the questions you chose with your partner, interview at least three unbelievers about your issue. (You and your partner can do this together or separately.) You can probably approach people in your office or call neighbors and say, "I'm taking a class where we're learning about different people's value systems. Can I ask your opinions on a couple of questions?"

Try to draw out the unbelievers' opinions on this issue by listening and asking further questions. The goal is to find out *what they think* and also the *basis* of their thinking. Don't give your own opinion unless asked. Instead, concentrate on listening and discerning. Don't feel awkward about writing the answers down. Most people enjoy telling what they think if they're sure you're not going to argue with them or sell them something.

Questions for Your Action Steps
The following are suggested questions for launching discussions about issues important to unbelievers. You will want to follow them up with more questions, particularly "Why?" or "Why not?"

Success.
1. What do you think it means to be a successful person? What would your life have to be like for you to feel really successful?

2. Do you feel like a success?
3. How important is it to you to be successful?
4. How do you feel when you fail at something? How hard does it hit you?

Work and leisure.
1. If you could spend your time doing whatever you liked, what would you do?
2. Do you like what you do for a living?
3. Why do you work? Do you have any reasons other than earning a living?
4. What do you like and not like about working?
5. How important is leisure time in your life?
6. What leisure activities do you like best? What do you like about them?

Children.
1. What do you think is the best part of having kids?
2. What do you think is the worst part of having kids?
3. What do you like best about your kids?
4. If you could learn to do one thing better as a parent, what would it be?
5. What would you like an expert on raising kids to explain to you?

Relationships with the opposite sex.
1. Think about the more successful man/woman relationships you know. Do you see any common factors that tend to lead to a satisfying relationship?
2. What do you think makes for a satisfying relationship with the opposite sex?
3. What ingredients do most people consider essential to a good relationship? How do you differ?
4. What do you think makes a good marriage work?
5. What influence did your parents' relationship have on your views of a good marriage?

Money and self-identity.
1. Do you believe money should affect how people feel about themselves?
2. a. What do you think motivates people to pursue money?
   b. If all those goals could be met in some other way, would money still have the value that it does now?
3. Do you identify yourself by what you own?
4. To what extent does your financial situation affect how you feel about yourself?
5. What five things are your most valued possessions? How would it affect the way you think about yourself if you lost them? Would there be a change?

Absolutes/right and wrong.
1. When you make decisions on moral issues, on what do you base your decisions?
2. Do you have some kind of standard or authority that you judge your life by? If so, what is it?
3. How do you decide whether a particular action you are considering is right or wrong?
4. Do you believe there are some basic concepts of right and wrong that remain constant throughout time?
5. Do you agree with recent court decisions that standards of morality are to be determined by the local community?
6. Do you think people have an inner sense of right and wrong?

BIBLE STUDY

Continue studying the issue you and your partner selected, using the questions and passages on pages 46-47. How is God's outlook on this subject like and unlike what you are hearing from unbelievers?

LOVE AND SELF-CONTROL

The early Christians were constantly forced to make decisions about disputable matters. In the course of dealing with many hot issues, the Apostle Paul framed two principles for handling them.

The Principle of Love

Jesus said God's permanent Law boiled down to two commands: Love God with your whole being, and love your neighbor as yourself (Matthew 22:34-40). So Paul told believers, "He who loves his fellowman has fulfilled the law" (Romans 13:8). Hence, when evaluating whether to do something not plainly commanded or forbidden in the Bible, ask yourself the following questions:

- Does this reflect my love for God? Or does it show that I love something else more? Can I thank God for this?
- Does this reflect my love for other people (my family, fellow believers, unbelievers)? Or does it show a disregard for them? Does it please me at someone else's expense?

In 1 Corinthians 13:4-8, Paul made it clear that by *love* he didn't mean a vague feeling. So we can ask ourselves, "Will doing this build up my nonChristian friend—drawing him toward Christ? Or will it confirm him in a life apart from Christ?"

We must also be concerned with what will build up fellow believers. Paul knew there was a kind of weak Christian who, when he sees you doing something he thinks is wrong, is tempted to imitate you and violate his conscience. For instance, say a believer has found that he is addicted to watching sports games on television. It's hindering his family life and his walk with God. Now, watching football is no problem for you, but it might not be loving to do so when this friend is around. We must ask ourselves, "Will doing this build up another believer, or will it tempt him to do what is wrong for himself?"

Paul also had run-ins with another kind of weak believer: the Pharisee. When this person sees you doing something he thinks is wrong, he is not tempted to imitate you. On the contrary, he is tempted to complain and judge. Paul *voluntarily limited his freedom* when the first weak believer was around, but he *refused to give in* to Pharisees. He graciously explained his convictions to them and pursued peace with them, but he would not conform to their standards. The gospel—love for the lost—was at stake.

The Principle of Self-Control

Paul's other principle was moderation, or self-control. Paul enjoyed lawful pleasures, but he would not let them take control over him. Anything that threatened to become an addiction was out. He wouldn't use a drug that fogged his mind and will. He had to be free to give up anything in a heartbeat if it hindered the gospel in some situation.

Love is patient, love is kind. It does not envy, it does not boast, it is not proud. It is not rude, it is not self-seeking, it is not easily angered, it keeps no record of wrongs. Love does not delight in evil but rejoices with the truth. It always protects, always trusts, always hopes, always perseveres. Love never fails.
(1 Corinthians 13:4-8)

Each of us should please his neighbor for his good, to build him up.
(Romans 15:2)

"Everything is permissible for me"—but not everything is beneficial. "Everything is permissible for me"—but I will not be mastered by anything.
(1 Corinthians 6:12)

Everyone who competes in the games goes into strict training. . . . I beat my body and make it my slave so that after I have preached to others, I myself will not be disqualified for the prize.
(1 Corinthians 9:25,27)

Strategies for Sowing the Word

Thus far we've been cultivating a friendship with an unbeliever. That's crucial. But if we never draw him or her to consider the Bible and what it says about Jesus Christ, we haven't done our job in freeing that person from prison.

Yet we can stop a friendship cold by suddenly preaching a sermon and calling for a decision. Our friend may have a lot more mini-decisions to go through.

So how do we start sowing the Word in a way that someone at -10, -9, or -8 can handle? In this session we'll consider three approaches.

WARM UP
(10 minutes)

1. When you solicited unbelievers' opinions this week, what did you *wish* you could say in reply to their answers?

> What people see must be verbally interpreted before the communication circle is closed. "How can I [understand] . . . unless someone explains it to me?" the Ethiopian asked Philip (Acts 8:31). We must talk about our faith.
> (Jim Petersen, *Living Proof*)

VIDEO
(15 minutes)

In this segment you'll get a review of cultivating and an introduction to sowing. You'll look at three sowing strategies:

1. *Raising the flag.*
2. *The faith story.*
3. *Suggesting a Bible study.*

As you watch, ask yourself this question:

How does each sowing strategy work?

TURN ON VIDEO

How not to raise the flag.

FROM THE VIDEO

It would be easy to get the impression that I am suggesting a sequence—that it's necessary to devote a period of time to establishing a personal friendship, so that eventually the person can be brought around to meet our Christian friends, so that finally we can say something to him. If I left you with this impression, I would lead you into a non-productive trap.

We can expect God to use us in all three ways *at the same time*. These three influences—our lives, the band of kindred spirits of which we are a part, and our words—should all be *sustained* until the person we are seeking to reach encounters Christ and moves into discipleship.

(Jim Petersen, *Living Proof*)

SOWING STRATEGIES

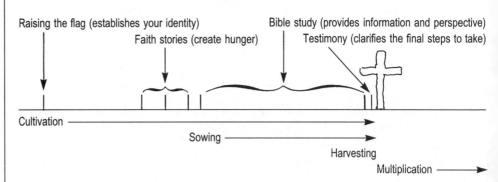

ON THE VIDEO

(25 minutes)

You've seen flag-raising several times now; here are a couple of examples:

> *Jackie (session 5):* "You wouldn't believe this, but we got it [insights on raising kids] out of the Bible."

> *Delores:* "I know it doesn't mean anything to you, Lydia, but it will make me feel a whole lot better if I can pray for you. That's okay, isn't it?"

Both approaches followed these principles of flag-raising.

Principles of Raising the Flag
- It should happen as a natural part of a conversation.
- It will create an opportunity (to tell your testimony and ask your friend for a decision) that you should *not* take advantage of unless the nonChristian clearly asks you to do so.
- If it takes more than thirty seconds, you're probably saying too much.
- Its purpose is to establish your identity as a member of God's family, not as a member of some religious denomination or affiliation.

---

2. Think of a conversation you've had with an unbeliever recently. How could you have raised your flag?

3. *(Optional)* What do you think would have happened if Delores had urged her friend to accept Christ or attend church, instead of just offering to pray? Why do you think that would have happened?

4. Bill told a faith story about how he discovered business principles in the Bible.

   a. How did that story affect Gerry? What mini-decisions did he make?

   b. What made the story work? What principles for telling faith stories can you draw from Bill's example?

A faith story gives a glimpse of life as a believer.

5. a. Bill didn't invite Gerry to investigate what the Bible says about business right away. Instead he said, "One of these days, if you want, I'll show you some of the stuff Tom showed me." It was only later that he asked if Gerry wanted to set a time and really do it.

   What do you suppose dropping the vague suggestion "one of these days" into his comment accomplished?

   b. Why might a study on business be a better start for Gerry than heading straight for a study on Jesus?

6. a. Which aspects of these sowing strategies strike you as easiest to do? Which do you feel you could handle?

   b. What aspects of these sowing strategies do you feel you couldn't do yet?

A few years ago, our family moved into a new neighborhood. . . . One of our first friendships was a young couple who lived down the block. . . . While we were out for dinner together one evening, my wife and I told them we were thinking of inviting some of our neighbors to discuss common problems in marriage, the family, and other human relationships, using the Bible as our basis. They reacted enthusiastically. The husband said, "I think we could get everyone on the block to come. We don't know of a single couple in this neighborhood who could be called happy."

(Jim Petersen, *Living Proof*)

LOOKING UPWARD

(15 minutes)

7. Get together with your action-step partner. For this exercise, one of you will take the role of the unbeliever and the other will play the believer. The unbeliever starts by stating what he or she believes about the issue you've been researching. (That opinion is based on the secular reading and the interviews with unbelievers.) A one-minute opinion is fine.

   Then the believer responds by explaining a biblical perspective (based on the Bible study he or she has been doing) in language the unbeliever would understand. The believer's goal is to respond in a short, natural way that's relevant to the conversation.

When he was thirteen years old, my son Todd asked, "Dad, how can I be a good testimony?" . . .

Finally I said, "Todd, don't worry about words. Just concern yourself with one thing. Be a peacemaker." I explained that if he would be genuinely considerate of the other person, and if he would take the initiative in resolving conflicts that arose, he would be doing what God wants of him. This was something my thirteen-year-old could handle.

A few weeks later, Todd had an argument with Eduardo, our neighbor's boy, and their friendship broke up. When Todd and I talked about the incident, we reviewed our discussion on being a peacemaker and read Romans 12:17-18 together. . . . Todd decided to take the initiative, visited Eduardo, and restored their friendship.

Soon after that, Eduardo's mother invited my wife over to her home to talk. She explained that her family had observed Todd's friendship with Eduardo and concluded, "We think you have what we need." A thirteen-year-old's life opened the door to another family.

(Jim Petersen, *Living Proof*)

For by the grace given me I say to every one of you: Do not think of yourself more highly than you ought, but rather think of yourself with sober judgment, in accordance with the measure of faith God has given you. Just as each of us has one body with many members, and these members do not all have the same function, so in Christ we who are many form one body, and each member belongs to all the others. We have different gifts, according to the grace given us. If a man's gift is prophesying, let him use it in proportion to his faith. If it is serving, let him serve; if it is teaching, let him teach; if it is encouraging, let him encourage; if it is contributing to the needs of others, let him give generously; if it is leadership, let him govern diligently; if it is showing mercy, let him do it cheerfully.

(Romans 12:3-8)

If you're playing the unbeliever, listen to how your partner responds to you. Would you understand that person's views without a church or biblical background? Is the believer responding to what you said, or talking past you? When the conversation is finished, exchange observations.

Then switch roles.

8. Close by praying for your partner. Ask God to equip your partner to raise the flag, tell faith stories, and eventually invite a friend to study the Bible. Pray for any specific concerns your partner is having about cultivating or sowing.

ACTION STEPS

Write a faith story. Think of a time in your life when a biblical truth made an impact on you. It might be as recently as today, when talking with your action-step partner gave you new insight into how to deal with an issue in your own life. Or maybe you made a biblically based decision some years ago about success or family.

You're not writing a testimony of how you came to Christ, but rather something like Bill's story of learning something new about business from the Bible. It might be a time when you changed the way you dealt with your spouse or kids. Or when you realized you were focused on the wrong kind of success.

Come to the next session prepared to tell or read that faith story. Write the story out or just jot notes—whatever suits your style. Be prepared to use language that an unbeliever would understand. No King James English, no Christian jargon (sin, righteousness, salvation, works, grace, Holy Spirit, etc.). The whole story should take less than two minutes.

Many people find it very hard to think of something God has done or taught them. But planning a faith story is a great chance to remember that you really have made some progress down the road with God, even if you're just a beginner in faith.

Pray. Of course, keep praying for the people on your TMWL.

MINI BIBLE STUDY

Read Romans 12:3-8. How should this truth about the Body of Christ affect the way you go about spreading the gospel?

For Further Reading
Jim Petersen, *Living Proof*, chapter 18.
Joe Aldrich, *Gentle Persuasion*, chapter 10.
Rebecca Pippert, *Out of the Saltshaker and into the World*, chapters 9-11.

Time and Teamwork

By now you may be saying, "I might really be able to handle this reaching-the-lost business if I had the time. But honestly, I'm up to my armpits in alligators already. If I add one more commitment, I'll sink."

God doesn't intend for us to sink. The time crunch can be dealt with. In this session we'll see that we can overcome stifling schedules and fragmented lives by

- clarifying our priorities,
- integrating evangelism into the activities of our lives, and
- teaming up with other believers whose gifts complement ours.

WARM UP
(20 minutes)

1. Let each person tell his or her faith story. After each one, the group members should offer feedback on how they think an unbeliever might respond to this story. Encourage one another—telling faith stories is challenging.

2. Right now, what aspects of your life get in the way of building friendships with unbelievers?

It's not about doing so much more than we're already doing, it's about doing more with what we do by including each other.

VIDEO
(15 minutes)

In this segment, our video group comes to terms with their crowded lives. When their usual meeting room is unavailable, Bill and Jackie find themselves hosting the evangelism group in their own living room. It's just one more demand in an already frenzied schedule. As you watch how the group learns to deal with the time squeeze, ask yourself,

How could I do what they are doing?

TURN ON VIDEO

YOUR NOTES FROM THE VIDEO

> The biblical pattern is for the individual's witness to be carried on within the setting of a corporate effort. The corporate witness says, "Look at all of us. This is what you too can become. There's hope." It's possible to discount or explain away an isolated individual, but it's impossible to refute the corporate testimony.
>
> (Jim Petersen, *Living Proof*)

The Great Co-Mission

Solutions for the Time Crunch
- Priorities
- Integration
- Teamwork

REFLECTING ON THE VIDEO

(25 minutes)

3. After watching the video, which of the following best reflects your current feelings:

❏ Frustration: I still don't see how I can integrate evangelism into my schedule.
❏ Hope: I'm beginning to see a glimmer of how it might be possible.
❏ Confidence: I'm sure I can fit reaching the lost into my schedule.
❏ Other:

4. Take five minutes to fill out the following chart on your own.

Areas of My Life Where I'm Already Involved With Unbelievers
Examples: *Designing project N at work; the PTA.*

Other Areas of My Life in Which I Could Include Unbelievers
Examples: *lunches; sports games with my kids; shopping; jogging or exercising; family excursions.*

Areas of My Life in Which I Could Not Include Unbelievers

5. Compare your answers to question 4. If you get new ideas from others in your group, write them down. Also, suggest ideas you've thought of on your own.

The video showed *believers* teaming up to accomplish what they couldn't do separately. This is the Body of Christ in action, each member doing what it was designed to do.

6. What team strategies for evangelism did the video portray? How did the teams cooperate in making the gospel attractive to unbelievers?

7. a. Below are some of the gifts needed for reaching lost people with the gospel. Take a minute to check the ones you think you have from God in some measure.

Gifts for Reaching the Lost
❑ Meeting people; making contacts with unbelievers
❑ Hospitality
❑ Building relationships
❑ Praying
❑ Explaining biblical ideas in secular language
❑ Leading discussions
❑ Organizing; coordinating details
❑ Serving:
  meeting people's physical needs
  listening when someone hurts
  making cakes
❑ Other:

---

b. Compare notes with the others in your group. What gifts would you add to this list? What gifts do you see in others that they haven't circled for themselves? How are your gifts complementary? If you were a team, how would you divide up the tasks? (In your list, jot group members' names next to gifts they have.)

LOOKING UPWARD
(5 minutes)

8. Of course, no one can do everything. God calls some people to focus their energies on raising up the saved through preaching, teaching, running the Sunday school, and so on. People called to church work can still invest in friendships with unbelievers and support teammates through prayer, but they simply will have less time to build bridges for the lost if they have to spend it on church committees.

To close, pray for guidance on these two issues:

One of the great life-revolutionizing benefits of becoming accountable to a few kindred spirits is the ensuing restructuring of priorities and commitments. . . . Another benefit . . . is the support it provides for overcoming the fears that always seem to accompany our efforts in evangelism.

(Jim Petersen, *Living Proof*)

One day, a couple of years after Mario had become a Christian, he and I were reminiscing. He asked me, "Do you know what it really was that made me decide to become a Christian?" Of course, I immediately thought of our countless hours of Bible study, but I responded, "No, what?"

His reply took me completely by surprise. He said, "Remember that first time I stopped by your house? We were on our way someplace together and I had a bowl of soup with you and your family. As I sat there observing you, your wife, your children, and how you related to each other, I asked myself, 'When will I have a relationship like this with my fiancee?' When I realized that the answer was 'never,' I concluded I had to become a Christian for the sake of my own survival."

I remembered the occasion well enough to recall that our children were not particularly well-behaved that evening. In fact, I remembered I had felt frustrated when I corrected them in Mario's presence.

Mario saw that relationships with Christ bind a family together. . . . [But] our family was unaware of its influence on Mario. . . .

We tend to see the weaknesses and incongruities of our lives, and our reaction is to recoil at the thought of letting outsiders get close enough to see us as we really are. Even if our assessment is accurate, it is my observation that any Christian who is sincerely seeking to walk with God, in spite of all his flaws, reflects something of Christ.

(Jim Petersen, *Living Proof*)

- Lord, what is Your commission for each individual in this group? To what extent do You want each of us to focus on equipping the saved to know and serve You? To what extent do You want each of us focused on reaching the lost? What gifts have You given each of us, and how do You want them used?
- Father, who is my team? Whom have You chosen to be my partners in fulfilling the calling You have given me?

CTION STEPS

Team up. During the coming week, talk on the phone or in person with at least one other person in your group about teaming up to reach the lost. (You could make plans right after this meeting to get together later.) Maybe you want to talk just with your spouse this week and work out the callings you sense from God. Maybe you want to get several people together.

The rules at this point are as follows:

1. Feel free to ask anybody, even someone outside the group.
2. Feel free to say no if asked.
3. Don't feel rejected if someone says no.
4. Saying yes to talk about teaming up doesn't lock you into being best friends with these people forever. You're simply exploring whether you have complementary gifts and interests, and how you might work together.

The topic for your discussion is: If we were a team, how would we go about helping the people on our TMWLs make mini-decisions on their way to accepting Christ?

Be sure to include prayer when you meet. Pray for the people on your TMWLs, and ask God to enable you to discern whether you should be a team and how you should proceed.

Pray. Of course, keep praying for the people on your TMWL.

BIBLE STUDY

We've talked about the gospel as seed we want to sow in an unbeliever's heart. But what is the gospel, the core truth we want a person to embrace? Look up the following passages and summarize their content.

- John 14:6
- Acts 2:22-39
- Romans 3:21-26
- 1 Corinthians 15:1-8

BUILDING A TEAM

Why a Team?
Our culture idolizes rugged individualism, but the Bible teaches corporateness—Christians acting as a body. David didn't drive out the Philistines alone; he depended heavily on the "mighty men" who fought at his side (1 Chronicles 11:10). Paul never took a missionary trip alone; the one time he had to

> Once you have prayerfully chosen one or more kindred spirits, the next steps are (1) to commit yourselves to co-laboring and (2) to take stock of your assets, putting them to work. This little team of two or more persons will serve as your vehicle for evangelism.
>
> (Jim Petersen, *Living Proof*)

Two are better than one,
   because they have a good return for
      their work:
If one falls down,
   his friend can help him up.
But pity the man who falls
   and has no one to help him up!
Also, if two lie down together, they will
      keep warm.
   But how can one keep warm alone?
Though one may be overpowered,
   two can defend themselves.
A cord of three strands is not quickly
   broken.

(Ecclesiastes 4:9-12)

Now to each one the manifestation of the
Spirit is given for the common good.
(1 Corinthians 12:7)

The body is a unit, though it is made up
of many parts. . . . If the whole body were
an eye, where would the sense of hearing be? If the whole body were an ear,
where would the sense of smell be? . . .
If one part suffers, every part suffers
with it; if one part is honored, every part
rejoices with it.

(1 Corinthians 12:12,17,26)

function without his team (Athens, Acts 17) was his least successful effort. And the only time the Bible says explicitly that Jesus spent a whole night praying w when He was selecting His team.

God didn't give any of us all the gifts or time necessary to do evangelism: building relationships, guiding people through the Bible, hospitality, coordinat- ing, making contacts with nonChristians, praying, serving personal needs. He designed us to function as a body (Romans 12:3-8, 1 Corinthians 12:7-26).

Instead of trying to do evangelism alone, try working together with your family, another couple, or another family. Involve your children in making con- tacts, helping to clean the house, making refreshments, and so on. Invite anothe Christian couple to a barbecue along with some unbelievers.

A team not only helps with the work, it also multiplies the witness. The Apostle John writes that unbelievers are convinced that Christ is who He says He is by seeing Christians acting in love and unity with each other (John 13:35, 17:23). Alone you could be considered a mutant, but unbelievers seeing two or more couples of caring, thinking, Bible-oriented people together will think it more than a coincidence. Yet, even if you are only jogging alone with an unbeliever, the spiritual support of others praying for your jogging companion multiplies the Holy Spirit's access.

How to Build a Team

What makes a team an effective commando unit rather than just a milling crowd? There are six essential features:

Common purpose (Philippians 1:27, 2:2). This is the cornerstone of effective teamwork. Too often teams flounder because their reason for existing is too broadly or vaguely defined. Once you've prayed and identified some like- minded people who want to explore the possibility of becoming an evangelistic team, spend your first meeting putting your purpose into words. Your purpose should be clear ("We understand it!"), relevant ("We want it!"), significant ("It's worth it!"), and believable ("We can do it!").

Appropriate division of labor. When a team breaks down a task and matches its component parts to the gifts and skills of the team members, it produces *synergy*; the whole is greater than the sum of its parts. The team becomes inter- dependent; every member's contribution is needed to fulfill the purpose. They are forced to cooperate.

Accepted leadership. Leadership provides the structure for cooperation. So, even though you are all friends and equals, you should definitely appoint one of your members as servant-leader. This person serves the team by coordination (When are the meetings? Who's keeping us on track? Have we dealt with all the issues?) and communication (Does everybody understand what's going on?).

Agreement on the plan. Whereas purpose deals with the what and the why of the team, the focus here is on the how. What will be the team's strategy for reaching the lost people on its heart?

Solid relationships. Interpersonal conflicts on a team are like friction in a machine. Solid relationships are the lubricant between team members. Members don't have to be best friends; the differences that enable synergism may preclude that. But the relationships should reflect trust, respect for each member's unique contributions, acceptance of each other's differences, and courtesy. Especially in the early life of a team, it is well worthwhile to give as much attention to building relationships as to pursuing the task. Get to know each other. Hear each other's story. Keep abreast of what each team member is facing in life. Pray for each other.

Good communication. Good communication is clear, open, and honest. It is the glue that holds the team together. If you don't know what someone else means, say so. And do your best to convey what you really think and feel when the group is making decisions.

For Further Reading
Jim Petersen, *Living Proof*, chapters 13-15.
Rebecca Pippert, *Out of the Saltshaker and into the World*, chapter 12.

Guiding Through the Scriptures

By now you've teamed up, integrated unbelievers into your lifestyle, and made some friends. You've attracted them to a biblical outlook through faith stories and natural discussions about life issues. You've brought up the idea of looking at a Bible study, and after a while, they've agreed.

Now what? What do you do when a horde of pagans arrives at your door expecting you to lead a Bible discussion that won't bore them? This session and the next will equip you to face that situation. This session will focus on

- choosing what to study,
- establishing a nonthreatening, nonreligious atmosphere, and
- avoiding Christian jargon.

WARM UP
(10 minutes)

1. What's the worst thing you can imagine happening if you hosted a Bible study for unbelievers? (If you can't select one worst thing, list some that would be in your top ten.)

VIDEO
(15 minutes)

In session 7, Bill invited Gerry to a morning Bible study on business. Gerry was interested but never got around to showing up. Since that video segment, things have shifted, and now both Gerry and Linda are coming to a couple's study just to kick around what the Bible says. As you watch how Bill and Jackie learn to launch their first Bible study for unbelievers, think about this:

What are the most important do's and don'ts for a Bible study with unbelievers?

We do not win people by proving to them that they are wrong. Rather it is the beauty and superiority of Christ that makes them realize there is a better way.
(Jim Petersen, *Living Proof*)

A nonthreatening atmosphere.

Christians should resist the temptation to "straighten out" doctrinal views of the participants which are not central to the issue of salvation. The issue is Jesus Christ, not infant baptism, total immersion, the inspiration of Scripture, pretribulationalism, or Post Toasties.

(Joe Aldrich, *Life-Style Evangelism*)

You know, you don't have to defend God. If they'll look at the Bible with you, the Holy Spirit will speak to them.

(Delores)

The Christian should refrain from bringing up all kinds of parallel passages. As a general rule the study should confine itself to one passage. Anyone can make significant observations on five or six verses. However, once the "resident experts" start spouting off other passages, the non-Christian realizes he is outgunned and out of place.

(Joe Aldrich, *Life-Style Evangelism*)

TURN ON VIDEO

FROM THE VIDEO

Elements of a Nonthreatening Atmosphere

Other Do's and Don'ts

Bringing the third supernatural resource into play.

REFLECTING ON THE VIDEO
(25 minutes)

2. What do's and don'ts for leading Bible study did you pick up from the video?

3. a. Review the mini-decisions listed on page 27. Which ones are you trying to help your friend make as you look at the Bible together?

   b. How should these goals affect the way you handle Bible study with him or her?

4. a. How do you feel about the idea that you don't have to defend God?

   b. How should this fact affect the way you conduct a study?

5. Why is it important to be content with only scratching the surface of a passage?

Jettison the jargon.

(Optional)
Christian jargon at best hinders communication of the gospel and at worst turns off unbelievers. Avoid it at all costs. As a group or on your own, come up with a clear, understandable synonym (a word or short phrase) to replace each of the following.[1]

born again	redeemed
saved	sin
lost	faith
justified	salvation
sanctified	repent
gospel	invite Christ into your heart

6. Steve offered this principle: *Jettison the jargon.*

   a. What did he mean?

   b. Why is that so crucial?

7. Why do you suppose Bill gave Gerry a Bible with the same page numbers as his?

8. What did you like about the way Bill launched the group discussion?

9. Do you feel you could handle leading or cohosting a group like that? Why, or why not?

(In session 10 we'll look at asking questions that produce a fun and effective discussion, and how to field questions from unbelievers.)

LOOKING UPWARD

(10 minutes)

10. Pair up with your action-step partner. Read over the action steps below and ask God how you should tackle them. Then discuss what you might do. To close, pray for your partner to be a light among the unbelievers he or she encounters this week. Pray about any obstacles in your partner's life that might make it harder for him or her to be a light (ask what those might be).

We strengthen our appeal immeasurably by letting [the unbeliever] know we intend to confine ourselves to an examination of the sole primary source that we Christians claim: the Bible. Although the average secularized person does not accept the inspiration or authority of the Bible, the idea of taking a look for himself at this famous book is likely to be attractive to him. It defines the parameters of the discussion for him, and for us. He thus feels that the odds are more even, that he will be free to think and decide for himself.

(Jim Petersen, *Living Proof*)

As a general rule, the Christian participants should avoid giving advice or sharing pious platitudes and spiritual bandaids. If they share, it should focus on their *personal experiences of the truth*, not an untested list from some seminar or textbook.

(Joe Aldrich, *Life-Style Evangelism*)

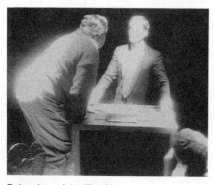

Relax. It won't be like this.

ACTION STEPS

Relate. Set a date to do something fun with an unbeliever as soon as possible. (If it doesn't work for this week, make it for next week.) Consider making it a foursome with your action-step partner and a friend of his or hers. If you decide to do it separately, be sure to get the date of your partner's outing, so that you can pray for him or her.

Before you go out with your friend(s), pray for opportunities to

• demonstrate love,
• raise relevant topics,
• ask provocative questions, and
• raise your flag or tell a faith story.

Then watch for and seize those opportunities as they come up. The issue you've been studying with your partner may be a good one to raise. See if you can still do most of the listening and offer your biblical view just to whet your friend's appetite. Share it as an opinion, not as truth, in as natural a way as possible, after you've listened to what the other person thinks. Try to tailor how you express your view according to where you sense the other person is.

Don't worry if this doesn't come off perfectly the first time. As you practice, you can refine your response until it is short, natural, relevant, and appropriate to the conversation.

Pray. Keep praying for the people on your TMWL.

BIBLE STUDY

Start reading through the Gospel of John. Get as far as you can this week. As you read, jot down what you notice about Jesus.

Jesus' Character and Personality

Jesus' Message

Jesus' Mission

Jesus' Identity

WHAT IS THE GOSPEL?

When Jesus interacted with people—whether His enemies, the multitudes, or His disciples—one issue dominated the conversation: *Who is Jesus?* If this was *the* issue for the people of Jesus' generation, it is still *the* issue in our generation. What is the gospel? The gospel is a Person: Jesus Christ.

But it's easy to obscure this message of Jesus' identity. We can do it in four ways.

The Gospel of Popular Issues

Sometimes a theme in the Scriptures so captivates us that we are tempted to make it part of the essential message. It might be God's love for the poor and oppressed, or His promise of prosperity to Israel, or His command to be stewards of the earth. Pretty soon we're proclaiming the gospel of social justice, or the gospel of prosperity, or the gospel of environmentalism, instead of the gospel of Jesus Christ.

The Gospel of Our Personal Emphases

Certain forms of expressing our faith become so natural to us that we can't envision a Christian functioning without them. We may think certain behaviors or doctrines are essential. But we must take care not to let anything—our religious traditions, our forms of worship, our personal doctrinal emphases, or our persuasions concerning Christian conduct—pull the Scripture out of balance and so restrict the gospel. We don't want people to reject Jesus because of our cultural wrappings.

The Gospel and Our Systems

Swedish youth are rejecting the Christ of the Reformation, the Free Church, and the Roman Catholic Church. They've never even encountered the real Jesus, who cannot be confined to a system. Did He become Protestant with the Reformation? Was He ever Roman Catholic? Does your friend have to become Baptist or join your "nondenominational" church in order to accept Christ? The answer is no.

The Gospel of the Christian Contract

Finally, we need to avoid focusing on the contract—how to transact a relationship with God—rather than on the person of Jesus Christ. We shouldn't become so intent on helping someone understand how to put his faith in Christ that we overlook the fact that he knows virtually nothing about Christ.

Instead of telling people what they need to do, we want to help them understand who Jesus is. As this understanding grows, it becomes obvious what one needs to do. Our friend often responds rightly without our help. If we focus on the response rather than on the understanding, we tend to force the contract. We lead a person to verbalize certain phrases, but he doesn't know what he is saying. The "decision" ends up having no effect on his life. But if we introduce him to the God-Man, Jesus, a relationship with Jesus becomes almost irresistible.

The Gospel of Jesus Christ

Once we accept that the essential gospel is Jesus, our approach becomes so simple. The question is, *Who is Jesus?* Take a look for yourselves, we tell our unbelieving friends. If you don't believe, we understand that. But let's go to the Bible with this single question and research the answer. You don't accept the Bible? We understand that, too. We'll just look at the Bible, and count on Christ's superiority to accomplish the rest.

"If you do not believe that I am the one I claim to be, you will indeed die in your sins."

"Who are you?" they asked.

(John 8:24-25)

The Jews gathered around him, saying, "How long will you keep us in suspense? If you are the Christ, tell us plainly."

Jesus answered, "I did tell you, but you do not believe."

(John 10:24-25)

When Jesus came to the region of Caesarea Philippi, he asked his disciples, "Who do people say the Son of Man is?"

They replied, "Some say John the Baptist; others say Elijah; and still others, Jeremiah or one of the prophets."

"But what about you?" he asked. "Who do you say I am?"

Simon Peter answered, "You are the Christ, the Son of the living God."

(Matthew 16:13-16)

The high priest said to him, "I charge you under oath by the living God: Tell us if you are the Christ, the Son of God."

(Matthew 26:63)

For Further Reading

Jim Petersen, *Living Proof*, chapters 18-20, 22.
Joe Aldrich, *Life-Style Evangelism*, chapter 9.
Richard Peace, *Small Group Evangelism*, chapters 4-8.

NOTE
1. Adapted from Will Metzger, *Tell the Truth* (Downers Grove, IL: InterVarsity Press, 1981), page 159.

Now, brothers, I want to remind you of the gospel I preached to you, which you received and on which you have taken your stand. By this gospel you are saved, if you hold firmly to the word I preached to you. Otherwise, you have believed in vain.

For what I received I passed on to you as of first importance: that Christ died for our sins according to the Scriptures, that he was buried, that he was raised on the third day according to the Scriptures, and that he appeared to Peter, and then to the Twelve.

(1 Corinthians 15:1-5)

"Who is Jesus?" is the watershed question. It will lie behind all of your questions about Scripture passages, and behind all of your friend's questions.

For instance, is God just? What about all the starving people in the world? Behind this question is the fact that if God is right, then I am wrong. If I insist that I'm okay, then God can't be okay. One of us is wrong. If God isn't responsible for the mess in the world, then it must be we humans who are to blame—me included. But once I accept who Jesus is, then I can face up to my own injustice. God's justice become obvious.

Does God exist? Well, if Jesus demonstrates Himself to be God, then God must exist.

(Jim Petersen, *Living Proof*)

Sparking Interest With Questions

Thus far you've invited some unbelievers (maybe just one) to a Bible study. Perhaps you're going to explore a topic like business principles or how to raise children. Maybe you're going to seek the answer to "Who is Jesus?" in a gospel. You've established a friendly atmosphere. What's next? In this session, you'll discover the following:

- why asking is better than telling an unbeliever,
- how to ask good questions so that the unbeliever can discover the Bible for himself or herself, and
- how to handle the unbeliever's questions in a way that maintains an atmosphere of safety and honesty.

WARM UP

(20 minutes)

1. Were you able to meet with any unbelievers this week? If so, what happened? Take a minute or two to share your successes and frustrations with the group.

2. Divide into pairs. One of the following passages from the Gospel of Luke should be studied by each pair. In your pair, read the passage and take three minutes to discuss this question: What does Jesus accomplish by using a question instead of simply giving the answer?

> A good question is the best possible teaching tool. Because Jesus was the foremost Teacher, no one could ask questions the way He could.
>
> (Jim Petersen, *Living Proof*)

On another Sabbath he went into the synagogue and was teaching, and a man was there whose right hand was shriveled. The Pharisees and the teachers of the law were looking for a reason to accuse Jesus, so they watched him closely to see if he would heal on the Sabbath. But Jesus knew what they were thinking and said to the man with the shriveled hand, "Get up and stand in front of everyone." So he got up and stood there.

Then Jesus said to them, *"I ask you, which is lawful on the Sabbath: to do good or to do evil, to save life or to destroy it?"*

He looked around at them all, and then said to the man, "Stretch out your hand." He did so, and his hand was completely restored. But they were furious and began to discuss with one another what they might do to Jesus. (Luke 6:6-11, emphasis added)

Once when Jesus was praying in private and his disciples were with him, he asked them, *"Who do the crowds say I am?"*

They replied, "Some say John the Baptist; others say Elijah; and still others, that one of the prophets of long ago has come back to life."

"But what about you?" he asked. *"Who do you say I am?"*

Peter answered, "The Christ of God."

Jesus strictly warned them not to tell this to anyone. (9:18-21, emphasis added)

On one occasion an expert in the law stood up to test Jesus. "Teacher," he asked, "what must I do to inherit eternal life?"

"What is written in the Law?" he replied. *"How do you read it?"*

He answered: "'Love the Lord your God with all your heart and with all your soul and with all your strength and with all your mind'; and, 'Love your neighbor as yourself.'"

"You have answered correctly," Jesus replied. "Do this and you will live."

But he wanted to justify himself, so he asked Jesus, "And who is my neighbor?"

In reply Jesus said: "A man was going down from Jerusalem to Jericho, when he fell into the hands of robbers. They stripped him of his clothes, beat him and went away, leaving him half dead. A priest happened to be going down the same road, and when he saw the man, he passed by on the other side. So too, a Levite, when he came to the place and saw him, passed by on the other side. But a Samaritan, as he traveled, came where the man was; and when he saw him, he took pity on him. He went to him and bandaged his wounds, pouring on oil and wine. Then he put the man on his own donkey, took him to an inn and took care of him. The next day he took out two silver coins and gave them to the innkeeper. 'Look after him,' he said, 'and when I return, I will reimburse you for any extra expense you may have.'

"Which of these three do you think was a neighbor to the man who fell into the hands of robbers?"

The expert in the law replied, "The one who had mercy on him."

Jesus told him, "Go and do likewise." (10:25-37, emphasis added)

Keeping a close watch on him, they sent spies, who pretended to be honest. They hoped to catch Jesus in something he said so that they might hand him over to the power and authority of the governor. So the spies questioned him: "Teacher, we know that you speak and teach what is right, and that you do not show partiality but teach the way of God in accordance with the truth. Is it right for us to pay taxes to Caesar or not?"

He saw through their duplicity and said to them, *"Show me a denarius. Whose portrait and inscription are on it?"*

"Caesar's," they replied.

He said to them, "Then give to Caesar what is Caesar's, and to God what is God's."

They were unable to trap him in what he had said there in public. And astonished by his answer, they became silent. (20:20-26, emphasis added)

Then Jesus said to them, *"How is it that they say the Christ is the Son of David?* David himself declares in the Book of Psalms:
"'The Lord said to my Lord:
"Sit at my right hand
until I make your enemies
a footstool for your feet."'
David calls him 'Lord.' *How then can he be his son?"* (Luke 20:41-44, emphasis added)

(Note: The Jews believed that no son could be greater than his father.)

3. a. Now gather together as a whole group and let someone from each pair report its findings.

   b. How would you summarize the value of asking questions?

VIDEO
(20 minutes)
In this segment we'll highlight good and bad ways to run a group discussion. Think about this question as you watch:

What are some basic principles of guiding a Bible discussion with unbelievers?

TURN ON VIDEO

FROM THE VIDEO

Basic Principles for Guiding a Bible Discussion

Avoid intimidating your friend.

Fielding Questions
- Clarify the question.
- Appreciate the questioner.
- Allow the questioner to save face, not yourself.
- Help your friend think his or her way toward Christ, even by asking another question, if necessary.
- If you don't know the answer, say so.
- Avoid giving your opinion on something the Bible doesn't address.

REFLECTING ON THE VIDEO

(25 minutes)

4. What principles for guiding a discussion did you pick up from the video?

5. Why is it usually more effective to ask what your friend sees in the Bible than to tell him or her what it says?

6. *(Optional)* From the video and your own experience, what do you think makes a discussion question good? (You might consider what you've liked or not liked about the questions in this discussion guide.)

A good question is one to which I don't know the answer.

A good teacher is someone who puts you in a situation that you can't get out of without thinking.

Simple Steps for Leading a Bible Discussion

The unbelievers' questions. Let's say you are leading a discussion of John 3:1-21. Don't ask people to read aloud, since many people find this embarrassing. Instead, ask your group to read the first paragraph to themselves and voice any questions it raises for them. Usually, unbelievers' questions are the ones most relevant to them. Sometimes no one understands the paragraph well enough to ask a question, but if they do, great.

Your questions. If an important truth remains uncovered in the paragraph after you've discussed the unbelievers' questions, you can ask your own. Bible discussion questions can have three functions:

- to *launch* a discussion on a subject (example: "What is John referring to when he speaks of 'the Word'?");
- to *guide* a discussion (example: "Why do you think He is described as 'the Word'?"); and
- to invite people to *summarize* the discussion (example: "What can we conclude about Jesus from this paragraph?").

Start with a launch question for the first paragraph, then ask one or more guide questions, and finally, ask a summary question about the first paragraph. Then move to the second paragraph. For each paragraph, your pattern will be as follows: (1) unbelievers' questions, and if necessary, (2) launch, (3) guide, and (4) summary. (Some paragraphs won't require a summary.)

7. Here is a launch question for John 3:1-2 (first paragraph at right): "What observations did Nicodemus make about Jesus?" What answers might you get if you asked this question?

8. With what guide question(s) might you reply to the responses you listed for question 7? (See the list below for ideas.)

Some Standard Guide Questions
• Why do you think he said that?
• What do you think he was getting at?
• What else do you see in this verse?
• Why do you say that?
• What do you mean?
• Why do you think he uses the word "_____" here?

---

9. The group should divide into subgroups of three. In your subgroup, make up two or three launch questions for John 3:3-9. Think about how a person might answer those launches, and plan some guide questions to follow them. Then think of a summary question that could tie together the discussion.

Launch:
    Guide:
    Guide:

Launch:
    Guide:
    Guide:

Launch:
    Guide:
    Guide:

Summary:

Some Standard Summary Questions
• How would you summarize the main idea of this paragraph?
• How would you say this in your own words?
• How would you summarize the idea we've been discussing?

Six Goals for Questions
• *Understanding*: What does it say? What else?
• *Interpretation or clarification*: What does this mean?
• *Justification*: How did you arrive at this conclusion?
• *Direction*: Mike, what do you think?
• *Comparison*: Where did we see this same idea before?
• *Application*: How does this affect us?

Now there was a man of the Pharisees named Nicodemus, a member of the Jewish ruling council. He came to Jesus at night and said, "Rabbi, we know you are a teacher who has come from God. For no one could perform the miraculous signs you are doing if God were not with him."

In reply Jesus declared, "I tell you the truth, no one can see the kingdom of God unless he is born again."

"How can a man be born when he is old?" Nicodemus asked. "Surely he cannot enter a second time into his mother's womb to be born!"

Jesus answered, "I tell you the truth, no one can enter the kingdom of God unless he is born of water and the Spirit. Flesh gives birth to flesh, but the Spirit gives birth to spirit. You should not be surprised at my saying, 'You must be born again.' The wind blows wherever it pleases. You hear its sound, but you cannot tell where it comes from or where it is going. So it is with everyone born of the Spirit."

"How can this be?" Nicodemus asked.
(John 3:1-9)

10. Now let one person volunteer to try out his or her subgroup's questions on the full group. The volunteer will ask his or her first launch question, and someone should offer a response. The asker will come back with an appropriate guide question, and so on. The asker needs to be sensitive to how the discussion is going. Is it time to go to another launch question? Is is time to summarize?

Take about five minutes on this, then applaud your volunteer and offer feedback as to how the discussion went.

LOOKING UPWARD

(5 minutes)

11. Pair up with a partner. Briefly tell each other one thing regarding a relationship with an unbeliever for which you'd like prayer. Then pray for your partner and for the people on your TMWLs.

ACTION STEPS

Pray. Keep praying for the people on your TMWL.

Practice a study. Meet with one or more people from your group this week for a practice discussion of John 1:1-14. For about fifteen minutes, one person should play the leader and the others, unbelievers. Then change roles. Aim for a forty-five-minute session. Use the launch questions that follow and make up your own guide and summary questions, or make up your own for all three. As you plan questions, remember that the core mini-decision you are working toward concerns "Who is Jesus?"

Launch Questions for John 1

The book *Living Proof*, from which the following are excerpted, contains launch (and some guide) questions for the entire Gospel of John, as well as guidelines for handling such a study. The notes are for the leader; the group won't have the questions or the notes in front of them.

As you become familiar with the process, make up your own questions for John, or another gospel, or a topical study, or anything else.

Read 1:1-14

1. What is John referring to when he speaks of the "Word" in verses 1-3?
   Note: See 1 John 1:1-3.

2. Why do you think He is described as the Word?
   Note: The function of a word is to transmit an idea. I say "pencil" and you know what I mean. I say "God" and what comes to your mind? From where did you get this concept of God? Jesus Christ is the "word" for God. (See John 1:18.)

   I am limited to the range of my five senses. Could God exist beyond them? Of course. If He remained beyond them, knowing Him would be an impossibility. Before I can know Him, He must take the initiative and give us the "Word." This is the claim made here about Jesus.

   Whether we are ready to accept this claim or not, we must admit that as long as the possibility of God existing beyond our five senses stands, the position of atheism or dogmatic agnosticism is untenable. Nobody knows enough to be either!

3. What are some of the qualities you see attributed to the Word in verses 1-5 and 14?

4. In verses 4-9, light is used as another analogy to describe Christ. What, to you, are some implications of this analogy?
    Note: See 3:19-21, 8:12, 12:35-36.

5. John 1:9 says every person is illuminated by Christ. In what sense do you think John means this?
    Note: All people are created by Him. All have *life* from Him. But man has abandoned the source of life and has fallen into darkness. There are still traces in man of his noble origin, but they are merely the remains of what he once was. What does remain?

    - *A certain God-consciousness*—Everyone has a certain knowledge of God, in the same way that something may be known about an artist by seeing his works. (See Romans 1:18-21.)
    - *An innate sense of morality*—Everyone has an idea of how life should work: the "internal laws." (See Romans 2:14-15.)

    These two elements explain the existence of religions and philosophies: a "God" notion and a standard of morality of which this God is the guardian. However, it is only by returning to the Light that man can be illuminated and thereby reoriented. Life is in Him. We understand life—our own and others'—by coming to the Light.

6. According to John 1:11-13, how does one enter God's family?
    Note: It does not happen through heredity, self-effort, or the efforts of another (pastor, priest, etc.). Only God can give life.

7. What do you think it means to "receive Christ"?
    Note: In 1:12, "receive" and "believe" are synonymous. In 3:36, the opposite of believing is rebellion against God—not accepting His authority over our lives. What do you conclude from this? *Believe* implies submission. (See Revelation 3:20.)

BIBLE STUDY

In these passages, is each person's barrier to following Jesus a matter of that person's mind, emotions, and/or will? Or a combination of these?

- Luke 8:4-8,11-15 (three sets of individuals)
- Luke 9:57-62 (three individuals)
- Luke 18:18-23 (one individual)

ANSWERING QUESTIONS

Acceptance

When a nonChristian begins to study the Bible with you, one of his or her biggest unspoken questions will be, "To what degree can I express what I really think with this person? How will he or she react if I express my true doubts and questions?" The person will first send out some rather "safe" trial questions. How you react to these questions will affect the quality of communication from then on. If you respond with dogmatism or defensiveness (both signs of insecurity), the unbeliever will quickly understand the rules of the game and proceed accordingly. He or she will either play by your rules or disappear. But if you show an attitude that encourages doubts and questions to surface, you will be much more effective. The unbeliever will get a chance to voice questions he or she has never had a chance to raise before. It almost doesn't even matter whether you have a clue how to answer the question, as long as you respond with acceptance.

Discernment
There are two kinds of questions: honest and dishonest. Dishonest questions intend to trap or embarrass, or to protect or justify the asker. Honest ones are for real learning.

Jesus answered questions according to their intent. When the lawyer asked Him, "What must I do to inherit eternal life?" Jesus knew it was a test, an attack, and He deflected it with another question. When the lawyer proceeded with a self-defense question, "And who is my neighbor?" Jesus replied with a story. But Jesus had all the time in the world for people with honest questions, like His disciples.

It's often hard to tell the motive behind a question. But a good test is to ask *yourself* (not the questioner), "What difference will it make if I answer this question? Will this person accept my answer and build on it? Or is this question really a statement of rejection?"

If the person asked the question simply to push you away or trap you, then you are wasting your time answering it. But often an unbeliever will start with trap and defense questions to see what you will do. So even when you discern that the question is not meant to be answered, you should still respond acceptingly.

If a question is honest, the person is usually willing to wait for an answer. He or she won't mind if you say, "That's a good question, but I don't know how to answer it at the moment. Let me study it this week, and I'll show you what I find out next time we get together." A person who wants to trap you will usually want an answer right away, but since the answer won't make any difference anyway, it doesn't matter if you don't know the answer.

Writing Down Questions
Questions that arise from the Bible discussion are usually honest and should be treated as they come up. But since nobody has all the answers, inevitably some questions will arise that you can't answer. That won't bother the other person if it doesn't bother you. To say, "I don't know, but I'll try to find out," will build, rather than undermine, credibility. Write down those questions and come back with answers when you have them.

Questions unrelated to the text require a closer look, however. If they are diversions to gain space, then give the person that space and let the Holy Spirit, not you, nail him.

An easy way to deflect trap or defense questions is to say, "Now that's an important question and we'll get to it. Let me write it down." Have the person repeat it so you can record it. This communicates that you are taking the person seriously. As you begin your next session, be sure you place that piece of paper on the table. This says, "I've not forgotten your question. We'll get to it, and if you have more questions, they're welcome, too."

Taking Questions in Sequence
The other reason for writing down questions is that sometimes they can't be answered out of sequence. (For example, how can you discuss the justice of a God whose existence is in doubt?) Frequently, the question "Who is Jesus?" needs to be answered before answers to other questions make sense. Explain this to your friend, and keep the list of questions handy to show you haven't forgotten them.

Of course, sometimes a particular question is really blocking someone's progress toward Christ. In that case you need to give even an incomplete answer to clear the road.

Sticking to the Bible
When studying with people who don't believe the Bible, it's crucial to consistently use nothing but the Bible. Your position is, "You don't accept the Bible's authority? That's understandable. But we're not here to discuss my opinions. We're here to let you judge the Bible for yourself. So when you ask a question, I'll try to restrict myself to showing you what the Bible says about it." Any other position undermines the Bible's authority, but this position lets the Bible function as the supernatural resource that it is.

For Further Reading
Jim Petersen, *Living Proof*, chapter 21 and appendix A.

Other Bible Studies for Evangelistic Groups
Design for Discipleship series (NavPress)
First Steps (Christian Business Men's Committee)
Jesus Cares for Women (NavPress)
Operation Timothy (Christian Business Men's Committee)

Making the Decision

When your friend is clearly attracted to Christ, it's tempting to push for a decision. But most people must travel a long road before they are ready to commit themselves to Christ; after all, their whole system of beliefs and habits has to be turned around. You can expect a long process, many disappointments, and some unattractive behavior because you are dealing with people who are spiritually dead.

What does it really mean for a person to accept Christ? And how can you play midwife to this spiritual birth, helping to bring about a newborn who is whole and healthy? In this session you'll

- explore the role of emotion, intellect, and will in a healthy conversion;
- see how to recognize which of these three is at work by the questions a person asks;
- learn when and how to give your testimony;
- discover the most effective use of a tract; and
- consider when to push for a decision and when to back off.

WARM UP

(15 minutes)

1. How did it go when you tried a practice Bible study this week? What did you learn?

2. Have you ever known someone who had made an emotional or intellectual commitment to Christ, but who didn't seem totally sold on it? If so, what was that person's spiritual life like?

VIDEO
(20 minutes)

In this segment you'll see how Gerry's emotions, intellect, and will all play crucial roles in his conversion to Christ. You'll also see how Bill takes all three into account as he answers Gerry's questions, offers a summary of the gospel, and describes how he made the final decision to follow Jesus.

As you watch, ask yourself,

What are the roles of emotion, intellect, and will in a person's decision to accept Christ?

TURN ON VIDEO

YOUR NOTES FROM THE VIDEO

We should expect it to take months, a year, or more of looking at the Bible before our friend decides that Jesus is God and that he will submit to Jesus as Lord and Savior. Remember the vast gap between where the nonChristian is and where he needs to be.

(Jim Petersen, *Living Proof*)

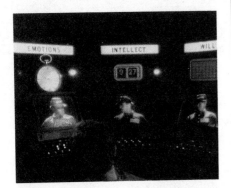

A healthy spiritual birth involves emotions, intellect, and will.

What is the role of
• emotion?

• intellect?

• will?

How does Bill use
• answers to questions?

• his testimony?

• a gospel tract?

REFLECTING ON THE VIDEO

(30 minutes)

3. What struck you about the way Gerry's emotions, intellect, and will interacted?

4. What would you say is the valid and necessary role of each of these in a healthy conversion to Christ?

   a. emotions

   b. intellect

   c. will

5. Over the course of his friendship with Gerry, how has Bill tried to overcome the resistance of each of these?

   a. emotions

   b. intellect

   c. will

6. Why do you think the will holds out longest against Christ?

7. a. Bill used the story of how he finally decided to accept Christ as an appeal to Gerry's will. What did you like about the way Bill handled that? Why was it effective?

   b. What do you think Gerry would have done if Bill had told that story six months earlier? Why?

8. a. Again, Bill used a gospel tract to summarize the decision facing Gerry. Why did Gerry appreciate this now, when he rejected anything that even smelled like a sermon a few months ago?

Ignorance is a serious obstacle to faith, but it is a secondary one. The real obstacle is rebellion. God wants us to put down our guns and come out with our hands up.

(Jim Petersen, *Living Proof*)

Keep working on your relationship between meetings for Bible study. Don't talk about religion or the Bible at those social times. You don't want your friend to start thinking you have a one-track mind and have stopped caring about him as a person. Talk about what interests him.

(Jim Petersen, *Living Proof*)

A real conversion happens when the will surrenders.

b. Bill gave the tract to Gerry to think about. He didn't press for a decision on the spot, but let Gerry go home to keep wrestling. Why do you suppose he did that?

9. The question of the intellect is, "Who is Jesus?" The question of the will is, "What does He want from me, and will I do it?" From watching Gerry, how do you think one can tell when an unbeliever shifts from the intellect issue to the will issue?

10. a. What part of Bill's approach do you expect will be hardest for you?

b. What further help could assist you?

c. What do you think will be the easiest parts for you?

Take cancellations and no-shows in stride. Don't show your disappointment, because that will put pressure on your friend. Instead, share your disappointment with your team and with God in prayer. Remember that your friend is still in darkness, and the world, the flesh, and the devil are all pressuring him to stay in his old ways and away from the Bible. Keep praying for him. Public opinion, misinformation, self-sufficiency, concern for position, and above all, rebellion are united to keep your friend from facing up to who Jesus is. Acknowledging His deity without submitting to His authority is admitting to rebellion, and that is a hard concession for your friend to make.

(Jim Petersen, *Living Proof*)

LOOKING UPWARD

(5 minutes)

11. Tell each other one aspect of this session's discussion that you would like prayer about. Maybe you'd like discernment to know when someone is ready to face the issues of the will. Perhaps you'd like skill and confidence in telling your story or summarizing the gospel.

Then pray. Thank God for one thing you've learned or one thing He's doing in you. Ask God to grant the requests of other group members.

ACTION STEPS

Write your story. Next time come prepared to tell how you finally decided to accept Christ in a one- or two-minute story in plain language like Bill's.

Pray. Keep praying for the people on your TMWL.

BIBLE STUDY

What would be some good reasons for separating new Christians from their old unsaved friends? What would be some good reasons for not separating from them? See Mark 5:18-20, 1 Corinthians 5:9-13, 2 Corinthians 6:14–7:1, and 1 Peter 2:11-12.

THE FOUR SOILS AGAIN

In Jesus' parable of the four soils we can see what happens when emotions, intellect, and will are not all involved in a decision.

Some people are like the path: "When anyone hears the message about the kingdom and does not understand it, the evil one comes and snatches away what was sown in his heart. This is the seed sown along the path" (Matthew 13:19). These people don't even have an emotional response to the gospel. Their only hope is for God to break up the hardness in their hearts—He does it often, and it's impressive to watch. Our chief job is to pray.

"The one who received the seed that fell on rocky places is the man who hears the word and at once receives it with joy. But since he has no root, he lasts only a short time. When trouble or persecution comes because of the word, he quickly falls away" (13:20-21). This person responds emotionally, but he does his thinking *after* making a decision. Then he has second thoughts, feels stupid for giving in to us, and avoids us. To prevent this miscarriage, we need to make sure that a person understands Christ and the commitment of faith before making a decision.

"The one who received the seed that fell among the thorns is the man who hears the word, but the worries of this life and the deceitfulness of wealth choke it, making it unfruitful" (13:22). This time the seed actually sprouts. Surely this time there's life! But only the emotions and intellect are convinced. The will is still attached to other commitments: wealth and the worries of life. This person has succumbed to our evangelizing because he has no good reasons not to become a Christian, except that he just doesn't want to. He's run out of arguments, but he hasn't really repented. There's no faith, no love for Jesus, just mental capitulation. We need to make the issues clear for this person: a decision on these terms is not what Jesus is after.

"But the one who received the seed that fell on good soil is the man who hears the word and understands it. He produces a crop, yielding a hundred, sixty or thirty times what was sown" (13:23).

For Further Reading
Jim Petersen, *Living Proof*, chapters 19, 22.
Joe Aldrich, *Life-Style Evangelism*, chapter 11.

Don't ask your friend for a six-week commitment to study with you. Take it one week at a time. The strength of your relationship and his interest in the subject matter should be what keeps him coming, not a promise he regrets. Pressure may make him flee or withdraw emotionally. The Scriptures and the Holy Spirit are pressure enough on his feelings and will.
(Jim Petersen, *Living Proof*)

Launching the New Believer

The healthy birth of a new child of God is a time for rejoicing. But what we do next drastically affects how fruitful the newborn will be as a servant of God. In this final session we will

- consider when to cut a new believer off from former associates, and when to leave those relationships intact;
- observe how to integrate the new believer into a vibrant community of believers for growth;
- discover how to promote multiplication through the new believer's network of relationships; and
- summarize our strategy for reaching the lost.

WARM UP
(15 minutes)

1. Give each person two minutes to tell the story of how he or she decided to trust Christ.

2. How did it feel to tell that story in two minutes? What did you learn? What would you do differently the next time with an unbeliever?

VIDEO
(10 minutes)

Last time, Gerry was struggling with whether to let Christ take control of his life, and Jackie was stunned to realize she was a Pharisee. This time you'll see how they resolve these struggles, and how Bill and Jackie's approach to launching a new believer affects Gerry and his unsaved friends. The strategy for reaching the lost will also be summarized. Consider these questions as you watch:

What happens to Gerry after he accepts Christ? What becomes his role in the evangelism strategy?

TURN ON VIDEO

FROM THE VIDEO

• How is Gerry integrated into a community of believers?

• How does Gerry become part of the evangelism strategy?

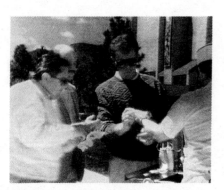

Every new believer is a link to an endless network of potential future believers. Don't cut those ties when you lead him or her to Christ.

ON THE VIDEO

(35 minutes)

3. What happened to Gerry after he accepted Christ? What became his role in the evangelism strategy?

4. a. What would be some good reasons for separating Gerry or another unbeliever from his prefaith friends?

   b. What are some good reasons for leaving those relationships intact?

   c. How would you decide whether to advise a new believer to separate or not to separate?

5. a. What has Jackie learned through her experiences with Gerry, Linda, and Raz?

b. Overall, would you say this experience has been good or bad for her? Why?

6. In the box that follows is a list of the main points made in this series.

   a. Which ones have you found to be especially valuable insights?

   b. Which ones still need clarification or practice?

Keys to Being Living Proof

1. There is a huge gap between the assumptions and values of Christian and nonChristian culture. We need to take a person's *culture* into account when we try to bring the gospel to that person.

2. However, all people have *built-in receptors* to the gospel: guilt, desires for love and significance, and fear of death.

3. Unbelievers are unable to make the first move toward Christ because spiritually they are *lost*, poor, imprisoned, blind, and dead.

4. God draws unbelievers to Himself through three *supernatural resources*: the Holy Spirit, the Bible, and us.

5. Evangelism is a *process* of guiding someone, in the power of God, to make *mini-decisions* on the way to choosing for or against Jesus Christ. Our tasks in that process are to

   • cultivate—prepare the *emotional* soil;
   • sow—plant the seed of the Word in the *mind*;
   • harvest—pick the crop, get a decision of the *will*; and
   • multiply—send people out to repeat the process.

6. We must make the first move toward the lost around us. We do this by establishing *common ground* on which to build a friendship. We address our friend's emotional barriers.

7. Being a good testimony is being light in a dark world and living with *grace* (unconditional, forgiving love) and *truth*. It is not flaunting our moral righteousness.

8. Early in our friendship, we need to *raise our flag* as people who base our lives on the Bible. We need to avoid raising a flag as members of a church or denomination, or as people who abstain from fun.

9. Living among unbelievers requires that we trust the Holy Spirit to deal

(continued on page 94)

(continued from page 93)

with an unbeliever's behavior, commit ourselves to please God rather than people, come to Bible-based convictions about disputable matters, and learn to say no gracefully.

10. We begin sowing truth when we tell *faith stories*—glimpses of what it's like for us to be believers, glimpses of biblical outlook. These start dealing with our friend's mind.

11. To be living proof of truth, we need to be *in the process of learning and applying* what the Bible says about lifestyle—relationships, money, priorities, and so on. We don't have to be perfect; it's the direction we're heading that counts.

12. The key to fitting evangelism into busy schedules is *including unbelievers in our ongoing lives.*

13. No one has all the gifts it takes to reach the lost. We need to work in *teams*.

14. When we've won our friends' trust and have intrigued them with our biblical lifestyle, we are likely to have success in inviting them to *study the Bible* with us.

15. A Bible study for unbelievers must be relaxed, nonreligious, fun, and nonthreatening.

16. The focus of the Bible study, whether topical or book-centered, is *"Who is Jesus?"* We may not be able to fix on this question immediately in a topical study, but our goal is to move toward this issue.

17. Asking and answering *questions* are our main Bible study techniques. We use launch, guide, and summary questions paragraph by paragraph, at about a chapter per session.

18. When we've satisfied our friend's emotions and intellect, his or her *will* still needs to be committed. We can confront this will by making the will issue plain, telling our own story of accepting Christ, and/or using a gospel tract.

19. Normally, a new believer should *maintain contact* with unbelieving friends. Instead of burning bridges with confrontation, the new believer should become *our partner* in cultivating (loving), sowing (studying the Bible), and harvesting old friends.

7. How do you feel about being *Living Proof* now? What questions or reservations do you still have? What positive feelings do you have? (You might review the list of fears and questions you made in session 1.)

MOVING FORWARD

(10 minutes)

8. What will you do next? Take a minute or two to think and pray silently. Write down what you would like to do next with what you've learned in this series. An action plan to consider follows.

    What I want to do next:

9. Share with your group what you wrote for question 8. Look for like-minded people with whom you might team up.

LOOKING UPWARD

(5 minutes)

10. Close in prayer, thanking God for what He's done in you through this series. Ask Him for the wisdom, courage, and strength to be *Living Proof* of who He is in your world.

An Action Plan for Getting Started
1. Find some like-minded Christians to make up your team. Discuss with them the principles of being *Living Proof*.
2. Pray together for God's help and guidance in becoming good witnesses for Christ. Ask God to help you clarify your priorities and integrate unbelievers into your lives.
3. Identify the gifts of each person in your team.
4. List some of the unbelievers with whom each of you has begun or can begin building friendships. Describe the relationships you already have with those people.
5. Commit yourselves to building relationships with those people. Discuss how you might integrate them into your lives. Look for ways to help each other overcome obstacles to making time or building friendships. Some possibilities include

    • throwing a party or game night with your team, and inviting each member's nonChristian friends;
    • pairing up with someone on your team to attend a sports event with some unbelievers.

6. Pray for each unbeliever on your list. Pray for each member of your team.

Probably the most dangerous thing about methods is that when they work, we begin to rely on them. We experiment with something. It works. We do it again, and again it works. As we become successful, we slip into thinking that continued success is a matter of just keeping that activity going. We feel that if we just repeat it long enough and hard enough, we will accomplish our goals. But when we transfer our confidence to such success-formula approaches, we are also resorting to carnal weaponry.

Our primary spiritual resources are the Spirit of God and the Word of God. Any true progress, any real spiritual victory, is gained through the power of these two forces.

(Jim Petersen, *Living Proof*)

LAUNCHING A NEW BELIEVER

Abandon Old Relationships?
After we lead someone to Christ, we are faced with two alternatives. We can inform our friend that now that he is a Christian he must abandon his sinful

lifestyle and stop seeing his old friends who may be a corrupting influence on him. If we get the new Christian involved in a lot of Christian activities, teach him to pray and study the Bible for himself, and replace his old friends with Christian ones, we may protect him from falling back into sinful habits. But we may also prevent a thorough inner transformation by imposing an outer conformity to Christian (but not necessarily biblical) standards. And we will force ourselves to start evangelism from scratch again. Worst of all, our friend may decide that while he likes Jesus, he doesn't like all the rules and activities of our church. Suddenly faced with the cultural chasm between the Christian and nonChristian world, he may decide to be a believer on his own without the Body.

Maintain Contacts?

The alternative is to encourage the new believer to maintain his contacts with unsaved friends. We will keep studying the Bible with him, and start teaching him to pray and to study on his own. We and the rest of our team will continue as Christian role models, encouraging growth in godliness. But he will be our bridge to begin evangelizing his friends. Like Levi in Luke 5:27-32, he will draw his friends first to meet, then to be friends with, and finally to investigate the Bible with our team.

This approach requires that we let the new Christian decide for himself about disputable matters (with our help to search out relevant biblical principles) rather than obliging him to conform to our church's norms about clothing, food, how to pray and worship, music, leisure activities, and so on. We have to be sensitive of how and when we integrate the new Christian into the corporate worship life of a church.

Training the New Believer

Unbelievers can be great evangelists as they invite their friends to "come and see" (John 1:46, 4:29). Even before he makes his decision, you can encourage your friend to introduce you to his friends. At social occasions, be just as social and nonreligious as when you started your relationship with your friend. Let his friends make the same mini-decisions as they observe your grace and love. If your unbelieving friend invites his friends to your Bible study, he can be a great help by making them feel it is safe to ask you hard questions. Make it clear that anyone can drop into your group at any time to check out what's going on.

New believers can be very bad evangelists—overbearing, dogmatic, pushy, unable to understand why their friends can't see what they have come to realize. Once your friend makes his decision, coach him on the process he went through and on the principles of being *Living Proof*. Teach him patience and sensitivity. Don't let the new believer bring his friends for you to evangelize; make him part of the team bearing witness. Have social time and study time with the new Christian's friends. Just as your original team gave the opportunity for corporate witness, sharing of gifts and tasks, and a forum for group discussions about felt needs, so too can the new Christian share in all of this.

For Further Reading

Jim Petersen, *Living Proof*, chapter 23 and epilogue.